TWISTED CROSS

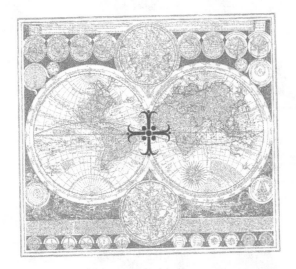

ADVENTURE TO THE NEW WORLD

Anita Perez Ferguson

Luz Publications

Twisted Cross: Adventure to the New World
by Anita Perez Ferguson

Published by:

Luz Publications
P.O. Box 90651
Santa Barbara CA 93190

ISBN 978-0-9673300-0-6

Publisher's Cataloging-In-Publication Data
(Prepared by The Donohue Group, Inc.)

Names: Perez Ferguson, Anita, author.
Title: Twisted cross : adventure to the New World / Anita Perez Ferguson.
Description: Santa Barbara, CA : Luz Publications, [2020] | Series: [Mission bells] ; [book 1] | Interest age level: 016-024. | Summary: "Salvador and his friend Blas are dragooned from an 18th century prison in Cadiz, Spain (1795). They are sent to colonial Mexico and later forced to participate in the Junipero Serra expedition to establish the missions of California"—Provided by publisher.
Identifiers: ISBN 9780967330006
Subjects: LCSH: Prisoners—Spain—History—18th century—Fiction. | California—Colonization—History—18th century—Fiction. | Forced labor—California—History—18th century—Fiction. | Hispanic Americans—History—18th century—Fiction. | Missions, Spanish—California—History—18th century—Fiction. | Young adult fiction.
Classification: LCC PS3616.E743 T95 2020 | DDC 813/.6 [Fic]—dc23

Printed in the United States of America

Dedicated to my lifelong friend
Patty, who always listened, enjoyed
and encouraged my writing.

Patricia Lee Finch Dayneko
1949–2016

CONTENTS

ILLUSTRATIONS

Adrienne Abate Kaplan, Illustrator

/

THANKS & ACKNOWLEDGMENTS

Thanks to my family; my husband Bill for his wise counsel, my sisters Sylvia and Patsy for their support and patience, and our great niece Casey Launer for her perspective and feedback.

I appreciate my friends Claudia and Patty, Doreen and Lois for their enthusiasm and insights.

For critical guidance and editorial support, I thank Naomi Eagleson and Mary Auxier at Artful Editor, Toni Lopopolo at Lopopolo Literary, Lisa Angle of Ninety Degrees Media and award-winning authors Mary Hershey and Dr. Geoff Aggeler.

Thanks to my early readers Penny Paine, Niki Sandoval and Judith Torres.

Technical and personal support go to Christine Nolt at Cirrus Book Design and Jennifer Newell at SB Creative Content.

Many thanks to the Santa Barbara Writers Conference and the Society for Children's Book Writers and Illustrators.

I appreciate the creative and conceptual work of Adrienne Abate Kaplan, Illustrator, and the expertise of our line editors Sonia Deninzon Green and Andrea Carnegie Chester and Dr. Alonso Benavides, Spanish Language Editor.

Ongoing thanks to my friends at Old Mission Santa Barbara for their faithful service and hospitality as well as their genuine reconciling outreach to the Santa Barbara Chumash Peoples.

CHAPTER 1

Spain 1790

A LONG WALK

The Devil whispered to Salvador each night. Huddled in a corner of the dusty inn, he sorted trash left by pilgrims on the road to *Santiago*, looking for something sharp so he could set a trap. The travelers crowded into a different broken-down inn every night. When the inn didn't smell too bad and appeared adequate, they pronounced, "God provides." If they said, "God gives us the strength to endure," the travelers were sure to face a miserable night. On the worst nights, Salvador managed to sneak away from the group, sleep under the stars and dream of new adventures.

"Send him home. I tell you, the boy's got the Devil in him," Brother Pablo said. Fidgeting with the knotted cord he wore around his waist, he pestered Brother Daniel, who led the congregation. The Easter pilgrims traveled from Salvador's *pueblo* home in *Yuste*, six hundred kilometers north to the Spanish *Catedral* at *Santiago*. The trip, meant to strengthen the faith of the believers, followed a historic route. Brother Daniel led every year, traveling the *Camino* and praying for his followers. His pale grey eyes looked straight ahead as he walked with confidence.

"Calm yourself, Pablo," Brother Daniel said. He held a prayer book shielding his words. "Salvador is only fourteen. I've heard his confession. Poor boy, one of Brother Santana's, uh, favorites. *Que làstima*, so sad."

"The little sinner will poison all the faithful. *Pobre Madre*, his poor mother, first her husband, now the boy," Brother Pablo said. He shook his boney finger in Salvador's direction. Salvador heard every word. Did everyone think Mamà a little saint with a ceramic halo? He often overheard gossip about his sinful father and holy mother. Had his confessor, Brother Daniel, told everyone about filthy Brother Santana? Salvador would find a way to pay them all back.

After thirty days of rain and mud on this

tiresome journey, the sky finally began to clear. With this promise of Spring and Easter, Salvador could last another day and make it to the *Catedral* with enough strength to run away from everyone, for good.

"Get away from the Brothers and away from your Mamà. She treats you like a little boy," the Devil's voice spoke to Salvador, loud and clear. "And far away from the reach of Brother Santana." Salvador slept in his only shirt for extra warmth. He shook out the dusty pants he used as a pillow every night. Rubbing his chin, he hoped to feel new stubble. Still as smooth as a baby's bottom. He pulled his ragged shoes from under his sleeping mat.

Mamà awoke too. "*Levàntate*, get up, *mijo*. We all trade a little pain for an eternity in paradise," she said. Mamà clutched her dark shawl around her shoulders. She never sounded like she truly believed in paradise. Each day she disappeared further beneath her shawl. How did she find her strength? Perhaps her strong will lived in her mission—to love Salvador into heaven.

Salvador's shoes flapped with separated soles. Hoping to make his Mamà smile, he walked in a squat, quacked, and shook the shoes in the air.

"¡Mira Mamà, un pato, look, a duck!" Why did he act so silly around her? No wonder she treated him like a baby.

"Oh, you foolish boy," Mamà laughed, shielding her broken teeth. She worried about Papá's punishments being revealed to others. "The birds are already calling you." A rude jay bird, carefully perched on a nearby cactus, squawked. "Take this and tie those shoes on your feet." She pulled a reed from the sleeping mat. When did she learn how to fix everything—mend a sock, cover a bruise?

"Listen, Mamà, I don't trust Brother Pablo," Salvador said. "Last night, I saw him pawing through unguarded packs." He tied his shoes on his feet. "He's got shifty eyes and filthy long fingernails." He hoped Mamà would believe him just this once.

"You were dreaming. He's just protecting us from contraband," Mamà said. "You know we walk to purify our souls, to ask forgiveness for our sins…and the offenses of others." Her voice dropped low as she ignored Salvador's complaints and muttered her morning prayers, "Nuestro padre, our Father…adelante, hurry Salvador."

"But Mamà, what sins do I have?" Salvador asked. A dark shadow of memory clouded his mind. "Brother Pablo reminds me of Brother Santana." Mamà didn't believe him when he complained about the Brothers. His friends understood the truth. They would laugh if they could see him trapped among this bunch of holy fools. The church expected the oldest son to accompany his Mamà on the Easter pilgrimage. Sal was the only son and this was the last favor he would do for Mamà. If only Blas, *mi compadre*, his best friend, had come along. He would listen and be on Sal's side.

Mamà unfolded a stained towel and recited a hasty grace before breakfast. "*Ahora comemos*, we eat now," Mamà said. She held out a bit of stale bread and cheese. What a meager meal to pray over. Salvador choked down the moldy offering. He imagined the Devil talking in his head.

"Make a real expedition out of this pilgrimage. Pay back the wicked Brothers." His crafty voice got drowned out by the next noisy family to awake. Feminine chatter filled the drafty room as the Mendez girls approached. A soapy scent preceded them. Their skirts and petticoats rustled as they moved. Salvador felt a rush of excitement. He imagined their long legs rubbing the fabrics beneath their skirts.

"*Buenos dias*, good morning Salvador," the girls said. The sisters swished, brightening the dingy inn. They attracted attention among all the pilgrims. Something about them, maybe the nervous way they made Salvador feel, told him these girls didn't walk this *Camino* to become holy. His eyes followed them as they jiggled their hips and posed for one another.

"Good morning," Salvador said. He pushed past the girls, embarrassed to be wearing the same dirty pants he'd walked in for weeks. He paused a moment to inhale their flowery scent.

"Nice shoes. Hey, it looks like your very holy pants got caught on the cactus," the Mendez girls said. They chirped like a trio of mocking-birds. More pilgrims (neighbors—young and old—from *Yuste*) filled the *sala*. They were all ready for the last day's walk.

The cactus! All morning he had looked for something sharp, some way to punish Brother Pablo. He saw the prickly pears near the trail last night. Salvador got an idea and rushed outside to find the bushes.

"*Bendiciones*, blessings on you, Mamà's boy,"

Brother Pablo said. Salvador brushed against him as he entered the *sala* meeting room, spreading the odor of his garlic sweat. He smelled as sour as his temperament. Salvador tightened his grip on his own knapsack and snuck past him, in search of the cactus. Brother Pablo pushed the others aside so he could stand in the center of the group. "*Atenciòn todos*, attention everyone. Tonight, our last night, we will perform a play. We shall enact the Last Supper," Brother Pablo said. He raised his arms dramatically as he spoke, then pressed his hands into a prayerful pose. Brother Pablo gave so many instructions to the group, Salvador could take his time to find the cactus. He carefully picked two spiny fruits, then dropped the prickly pears into his knapsack and headed back into the *sala*.

"Guadalupe, you represent Mary Magdalene," Brother Pablo said. Mamà blushed and covered her face, thrilled to have the role of Mary, the mother of Jesus. Brother Pablo corrected her, "No, not the Holy Mother. You play Mary the harlot, who washed Jesus' feet with her hair.

"Mary is a good role, Mamà," Salvador said. He stood behind her for support—faking a smile, gritting his teeth. Brother Pablo named all the roles before embarrassing Salvador.

"You will play the part of Judas," Brother Pablo said. This shocked the entire group of travelers, who took a step away from Salvador.

"*¡Ay Judas!*" the Mendez girls squealed in horror. No one wanted to stand near the traitor who betrayed Christ. Salvador imagined throttling Brother Pablo on the spot. Instead, he clenched his fists and bit his lip.

"*Bueno*, whatever you say, but I can't make the walk until I find my bag. Mamà's golden earrings are in the bag and it is lost," Salvador said.

Mamà leaned toward him to whisper, "*¿Qùe oro*, what gold?" Sal watched Brother Pablo take an interest in the lost bag with gold earrings. He planned to teach Brother Pablo a painful lesson.

After the evening meal, Salvador played the part of Judas and Mamà pretended to wash Jesus' feet with her hair. Brother Pablo could not direct his play or even watch it. He paced outside, grumbling about his bandaged, aching hands—swollen and full of cactus spines.

—✳—

CHAPTER 2

Santiago, Spain 1790

REVENGE

The next morning the weary pilgrims dragged their feet as they neared the *Catedral* of *Santiago*. Desperate to get to the front of the line, Salvador darted ahead of the other travelers, skipping over pie-sized animal droppings in the path.

"*¿A dónde vas*, where are you going?" Mamà asked. Salvador wanted to get away from everyone, especially his mother's constant watch.

"We all go faster when we help each other," Brother Daniel said. Where did he come from? Daniel, the one decent Brother, carried a heavy bundle for another traveler. Daniel's long confident stride seemed easy compared to Salvador's feverish scramble.

"*Cálmate hijo*, calm down son, even a great

actor helps to carry the props," Brother Daniel said. His long strides made the walking seem rhythmic. How could he be so good, so different from Brother Pablo and Brother Santana?

"I'm no actor," Salvador said. He didn't want to be teased about his role as Judas.

"I know, you are not really an actor, and you are certainly not Judas. Give me some help here," Brother Daniel said. He lifted his package toward Salvador. His hands were strong and clean, but Salvador noticed his filthy ragged robe dragging in the dirt.

"I'm not helping anyone. Isn't it true we all make our own way?" Salvador asked. He watched to see how the Brother reacted.

"Why make this journey if that is what you truly believe, my son? We are all meant to help the others on the road," Brother Daniel said. Salvador noticed his annoying habit of answering a question with another question. "You are excited to see the *Catedral*, no?"

"I'm not looking for any stupid relics or any 'love thy neighbor' preaching. I only want to see the riches of *Santiago*," Salvador said. Would he be punished for speaking honestly? "Is it so bad to want wealth and new experiences—a clear path, a clean bed, even a clean robe?" He tested Brother Daniel's patience, *¿y por qué no?* he'd soon escape the control of the Brothers.

"Is this the only prayer you take with you into the *Catedral*?" Brother Daniel asked. "What if God has a job waiting for a strong, honest boy in *Santiago*? Would that be enough of a new experience for you?"

Salvador watched him closely. Did Brother Daniel make fun of him? Sal wanted to be good, but every time he tried, someone, like Brother Santana, hurt him. Could God really understand the pain in his heart and still have use for him? He moved ahead of Brother Daniel. After one more hour on the road, he would enter *Santiago*. He only wanted to get away from everyone who knew him and start his own life of adventure.

Once inside the city limits, the pilgrims joined the traders, Brothers, soldiers and sailors in the streets and plazas of *Santiago*. Somehow, Mamà found Salvador lurking near the *Catedral*.

"Stay close to me, *mi amor*, my dear," Mamà said. She led him back to the *Catedral's* stone barricades with the other travelers. "*Mucha gente*, too many people, I might lose you in this crowd," Mamà said. She waved her hand in the air to push away the sour smells from the mobs of pilgrims, dirty after forty days of the walking pilgrimage. Pairs of uniformed military men patrolled back and forth inside the barriers to control the crowd.

"As soon as I get in the church, I'll touch the silver *Botafumerio*," Salvador said. This was the gigantic silver incense container used to rid the church of the pilgrims' stench. It was the only relic Salvador wanted to see and touch.

"Step over here, *mijo*, son," Mamà said. "Let the Brothers enter first."

"Kneel, kneel!" the soldiers said as they pushed the crowd back. People ahead of Salvador bowed on the ground.

"Why let those Brothers enter ahead of us?" Salvador asked. "It's not fair, we walked all this time!"

"¡*Cállate* boy, hush!" Mamà said. On her knees, she reached out to kiss the hem of the Brother's robes.

"No, Mamà, we don't need their blessings," Salvador said. Among the unruly crowd, he spotted familiar faces. "I know for certain, two of those Brothers are no more holy than me."

He saw Brother Pablo, who taunted him on the road to *Santiago*. Behind him, Salvador spotted Brother Santana, his abuser from *Yuste*. His body went stiff with fear and hatred. Clean white religious vestments disguised the dirty Brothers. They pushed ahead of everyone and entered the *Catedral*.

By the time Salvador and Mamà got inside, the service was half over. The *Catedral* ceiling seemed higher than the mast of a ship. Tall stained-glass windows reflected dazzling colors all the way to the floor. He promised Mamà he would take communion and drink from the sacred silver cup, so Salvador moved toward the altar rail. Thirsty worshipers pushed him forward. The silver incense container swung out of his reach.

"*Paz de Dios*, the peace of God," Brother Santana said. He gripped the silver chalice, full of wine, the color of his ruby ring. At that moment, Salvador realized, Brother Santana never got sent away or punished for his abuse of Salvador and his friends. They only sent him to a new church, this fancy *Catedral* in *Santiago*. A familiar voice, *El Diablo*, the Devil, whispered to Salvador.

"Now's your chance to pay him back," the Devil said. Salvador's heart raced. Santana never paid for his abuses, but Salvador paid with his soul. He remembered the ruby ring and those beady eyes that still haunted his nightmares. The *Catedral's* heat and odors made it hard to breathe. He pushed back against the crowd and rammed his elbow into the cup of wine held by Brother Santana. Bright red wined dripped all over the Brother's clean white vestments. It only seemed right that Brother Santana's robes were ruined after he stained the lives of many young boys in *Yuste*. Now he stared at Salvador, casting an evil spell on the boy. Salvador panicked and pushed through the crowd toward an arched doorway opening onto the plaza. He escaped from the stench of the *Catedral* to breathe in the cool air in the plaza. His heartbeat fast, pulsing with anger and sorrow.

The Devil kept chattering as Salvador tried to calm himself. "This will be your last mass, Salvador. You have another fate," he said. What fate? Salvador's questions were drowned out by calls from boisterous sailors filling the plaza.

"Fetch me a brew, boy, *por un peso*, here's a dollar," a sailor said. He staggered toward

Salvador and tossed the money at his feet. Throngs of seamen filled the plaza between the church and the port road to *Finisterre*. They stomped around like wild bulls, cursing, gambling and wrestling with one another.

"¿*Solo uno* just one?" Salvador asked. He grabbed the money. Should he trust this man?

"¡*Ha, miralo!* Look here, we're joined by a little businessman tonight," the sailor said. He tossed more money and pushed Salvador toward a cart filled with beer barrels. Salvador actually held real silver pesos! These husky men looked rich and tough in their high leather boots and their heavy capes slung over their backs. Each man wore a golden emblem on a chain and a sword hung from his belt. Returning with the beer, Salvador asked about the golden emblem.

"¿*Este*, this? It's the symbol of our ship, *La Buena Fortuna*, the Good Fortune," the sailor said. Most of the men ignored Salvador, but a few gave him a nudge and a wink, making him feel welcome. The more they drank, the more stories and silver they shared with him. Salvador's wish for adventure was already starting to come true.

After hours of fetching countless beers and

hearing endless stories, Salvador collapsed on a cargo bag to sleep under the beer wagon. He completely forgot that he sat just a few yards from the *Catedral*. His dreams were interrupted at midnight.

Mamà discovered him curled up in the damp plaza. "*Mijo, ¡gracias a Dìos!* Thank God, you are all right!" Mamà said. She recaptured Salvador, covering him with her shawl.

"Don't fuss, Mamà! *Estoy bien*, I'm okay," Salvador said. The plaza looked so empty. Did he only dream about the sailors? He secretly fingered his collection of new silver coins in his pocket.

"God's mercy led us to you, my son. Ready to come now?" Brother Daniel asked. He leaned over Salvador and tried to pull him to his feet.

"Where are the vendors and the sailors?" Salvador said. "I'm staying here. I have a job, and real silver, too." Once again, just to be sure, he jangled the coins in his pocket.

"You are all alone out here," Brother Daniel said. He heard the coins jangling. "A job, you say? I think protecting your Mamà on the long walk back to *Yuste* is your job." Did the Brother guess something important happened to Salvador?

"You can tell me all about last night's adventure as we walk."

"Is there really danger on the way home?" Salvador asked.

"¡Si mucho! Thieves ambush returning pilgrims to steal their silver," Brother Daniel said.

"Why does Mamà need me to protect her?" Salvador asked.

"We need a man like you to help us. Brother Pablo will stay behind," Brother Daniel said. "His hands are mysteriously infected."

"He is not going back?" Salvador asked. Was this just a trick to get him to return to *Yuste*?

"He will stay here with Brother Santana, who somehow fainted during the mass last night and dropped the Holy wine," Brother Daniel said.

Salvador heard the results of his actions, held back a grin and felt a twinge of guilt.

"You may not believe me, but we must all answer for our lives at the end of the journey. Let's leave them behind and walk with those who need our help," Brother Daniel said.

CHAPTER 3

Five years later...
Yuste, Spain 1795

RESCUE

"Is this the first time you've been in a church since you visited *Santiago* with your Mamà?" Blas asked. Almost right, five years ago, on the *Santiago* pilgrimage, Sal rejected the Church. Sal and Blas staggered away from a wedding reception for school friends in *Yuste*. Barely eighteen, Sal and Blas were ready to begin their life quests. But their friends seemed to be in a rush to become old men—husbands and fathers in a village of nobodies.

"Why are you still so bitter about the trip, Sal?" Blas, *chismoso*, chattered when he drank. At least the modest wedding offered a chance for plenty of free alcohol. Sal and Blas attended many such gatherings. They had a standard routine, drink several toasts to the unhappy couple then leave quickly. They knew if they stayed too long, the old women would try to drag them toward the young women who were hungry for marriage. Neither Sal nor Blas planned to marry soon. They escaped the gathering and continued to talk.

"How long since your Mamà died? May she rest in peace," Blas said.

"*Tres años*. I went to her funeral three years ago," Sal said. A painful memory of how badly he treated Mamà during the pilgrimage stuck with him. After they returned to *Yuste* a deadly fever took her life. Why did Blas have to mention her? If Blas wanted to relive dark memories, Sal could share plenty.

"Ha, did I ever tell you who served communion in *Santiago* so many years ago? That demon, Brother Santana. You remember him?" Sal asked.

"I wish I could forget him, we all do," Blas said. "You crashed in and saved me when Santana planned to give me special sanctions for service," Blas said. Sal made sure Blas never stayed alone with Brother Santana again. They avoided talking about it but kept watch over the younger boys until Brother Santana left their church in *Yuste*.

"Yeah, now I know they just moved him to another parish," Sal said. He remembered saving Blas from Santana, but he wondered if Blas really understood what Santana intended to do to him. "Brother Santana wasn't the only bastard in *Santiago*. I kept watch on another sneaky Brother the whole trip." He remembered the one good man, Brother Daniel. Why weren't there more like him? No matter how disappointing the pilgrimage was, it held the first excitement in his life. He also recalled the Mendez sisters and the sailors in *Santiago*. As he walked with Blas, he glanced around his own shabby town, *Yuste*; a town so small they knew the names of all their neighbor's dogs. Would he ever get away?

The boys reached Sal's house and discovered his Papá packing boxes and bags. "Grab those tools. Leave the rest of this junk behind," Papá said. "I've got a new job in *Cadiz*." Sal never saw his Papá move so fast. He tossed everything in piles, anxious to get them moved out of the house.

"But, but what about Mamà's stuff?" Sal asked. "You want me to leave it here?" Papá never talked about Mamà's death or let Sal talk about how much he missed her. Papá never talked about anything.

"*Estùpido*. She's not going to use it anymore," Papá said. How coldly he spoke of Mamà.

Why did he want to move five hundred kilometers south for some new job? Who did Papá know in *Cadiz*? Sal wanted to get out of *Yuste* too, but this unexpected news sounded suspicious. Is Papá running away from someone or something?

"Okay, take her old shawl if you need something to hold on to," Papá said. "Sometimes, you are more like a little girl than a young man." Sal still felt like a little boy, but he had to pretend to be a man. Already eighteen, he sounded like a child asking Papá too many questions.

"Can Blas go with us?" Sal asked. His friendship with Blas, whose family always lived and worked nearby, made life bearable.

"Yeah sure, bring him if you want. He's a good kid," Papá said. "Maybe my new boss will have work for all three of us." Papá's sly smile made the trip seem all the more suspicious. By twilight, the three of them were walking on the road toward *Cadiz*. "*Vàmanos*, hurry," Papá said. Salvador and Blas trailed behind. They were smart enough to keep quiet until they walked alone.

"I don't know why he's making this sudden move. We've never gone to *Cadiz* before," Sal said.

"Maybe he just wants to get a fresh start. Too many sad memories at home," Blas said. Sal doubted that; his Papá never acted sentimentally. They were on the road for seven long days. Papá trudged forward like a *burro*, a donkey. After a day's walk, he drank his night away. What were they really heading toward? Sal expected to see one long beach when they reached *Cadiz*, but the place seemed to be a puzzle of alleys and roads leading to the port. Like most of the other southern towns in Spain, North Africans—Moors—with black faces, turbaned heads and thick accents congregated in the streets. Papá seemed to know his way around the neighborhoods.

At the end of a narrow alleyway, he disappeared behind a low wall. Not really a barrier, just a pile of stones and a collection of rubbish. Even the gate was only a few twigs tangled in a low opening.

"*Espèrame*, wait here," Papá said.

"What's over there?" Sal said. The boys peered

through the gate toward a sandy slope with a crooked house on one side.

"Just a shack and a bunch of children running around," Blas said. "Hey, one boy looks a lot like you, but younger." They spotted a woman cooking over an open fire pit. Were these all of her kids? "She's hugging him! *Mira*, look, your Papá knows her," Blas said. As soon as he said this, Sal looked away.

"Papá never talked about having a sister or anyone in *Cadiz*," Sal said. Could this be the family his parents had argued about—Papá's horns and tail? Sal didn't want to see any more. "Let's get some rest," Sal said. He let Mamà's shawl fall to the ground. He and Blas laid down and leaned their heads against the rocks.

The next morning Papá roused the boys early to roam the docks and look for work. He didn't even bother to mention the phony job or his other family. He lied about everything. He even dared to ask the boys to reinforce the gate where they slept.

"How many days do we look for work?" Blas said. He spoke quietly to Sal, not wanting to confront Papá. "I thought he had a job here?"

For three nights, the boys slept huddled

against the rocks near Papá's other family. Realizing the truth of the move, Sal got up at dawn, eager to get to the dock. The ships and sailors reminded him of his time in *Santiago*. He covered his hurt and anger by making his own plans. Why not? Papá only brought them here as extra laborers for his second family.

"You go back home if you want, Blas," Sal choked out his words, his head hung low. "But I'm thinking of a scheme for the two of us to get out of here." He felt lousy and abandoned by his own father. "Papá made no explanation about this family in *Cadiz*. He lied about having a job here so we'd join him on the road trip. *Olvídese*, forget it— forget him!" Sal said.

"Sorry, Sal, but I'm not too surprised," Blas said. He turned his face away from Sal. "I thought you knew all about the rumors of your Papá and his other women. I've heard them ever since we were boys." He turned back to face his best friend, "Tell me about your plans," Blas said. He always relied on Sal for the best plans and schemes.

"Did you see the huge ships entering the port today?" Sal said.

"You mean those Portuguese slave ships?" Blas

said. The slave ships were notorious; huge and guarded day and night by men who looked more like thugs than sailors.

"No, idiot, I mean our own Spanish galleons, loading tons of supplies for the New World," Sal said. He could face anything as long as his friend Blas stayed with him. "This plan will work. Hear me out." Now he had Blas's full attention. "Yesterday, in the dock beyond the jail yard, I saw one of the King's galleons stuffed full of food." He waved his arms, acting out each stage of his plan for Blas. "If I can distract the stevedores stacking the supplies before they get hoisted into the galleon, you can snatch the food!" The boys talked all night, sketched out the dock and their escape route with a stick in the dirt and hardly slept a wink. The next day Sal's scheme did not go as planned.

"Forgive me, Blas, please move. Say something," Sal said. "*Lo siento*, sorry, sorry, sorry," he muttered. It was his plan that landed them both in this rat-infested jail. His best friend lay curled on the filthy floor next to him. Badly beaten, Blas struggled for his life.

"They only keep prisoners here for seven days. The guy in the next cell said so," Sal said.

"You can hold on." Blas did not move. Sal could do nothing for him but blabber on and try to sound hopeful. "He also told me first-time prisoners give *los ratones*, the rats, names! Can you believe it? I named this rat Chaco," Sal said. To keep from going crazy, he turned to talk to the little brown rodent. He desperately wanted someone to talk to. At least Chaco listened.

"Chaco, I know where to find a big block of tasty cheese, *queso*," Sal said. His mind ran in circles thinking how his plan went so wrong. Like some *loco*, a crazy man, he talked to a stupid rat. Chaco ran in circles too, his whiskers twitched. "My part worked perfectly. But my fat friend here stumbled during the getaway. Beaten, then arrested, now we are stuck in this tiny cell with you, little whiskers."

Sal didn't mean to put all the blame on Blas. He talked to the rat instead of looking at his friend. Blas, usually ready with a song or a joke, looked so bad that Sal hardly recognized him. His eyes bruised, his lips swollen shut—maybe one of the old stories would rouse him.

"*Señor Chaco*, I will tell you a story about our Papás. *Sì, sì*, they were friends, too, and told us many tales when we were boys," Sal said. "Stories about their work as blacksmiths for *El Rey*, the King." He checked to see if Blas was still breathing, then continued in a whisper. "Their ironwork filled the King's royal palace. They made candelabras used for the holy mass and enormous bells rung for missionaries who crusaded round the world. We believed every word they said." Blas would not respond. Sal felt so guilty he continued telling stories to the rat.

"Be careful, Chaco. Believe only half of what you see, none of what you hear. *En verdad*, in truth, our fathers barely scraped by as lowly blacksmiths." He stood and stomped around the tiny cell. "*Nuestra España*, our Spain, holds nothing for the low born, like you, me and Blas lying here." Chaco cut off the conversation. The rat scampered away through a crack in the wall. Sal's stories stopped, and with them, the memories of his boyhood full of dreams.

Jailed in *Cadiz, Spain*

CHAPTER 4

Cadiz, Spain 1795

SEA VOYAGE

Chaco, the rat, reacted to noise in another part of the jail and ran away. Someone stomped through the cell block, barking orders to the jailers. The noises came closer to Sal and Blas's cell.

"This one! Over here, him," a big man in a military uniform said. The jailers clamped iron shackles on Sal's wrists and pulled him away from Blas.

"*Adios, mi hermano*, goodbye brother," Sal said. Blas twisted toward him and moaned. A soldier stepped into the cell and yanked Blas's head, then slapped his face.

"What's wrong with this man?" he asked. Blas, now wide awake, grunted and spat in the man's face. This would get him killed for sure.

"Calm yourself, *peon*," the soldier said. "This one's strong. Put him in shackles and move him out."

Strong enough for what, Sal wondered? The guards shoved them both outside to the jail yard and left them squinting in the blazing sun. The white walls around the yard, smeared with dark dripping stains, looked like a place for firing squads. Sal heard a faint prayer chant. A huge St. Peter, draped in a shining robe, appeared in the yard between two monks. Was this their moment of execution?

"Blas, brace yourself, *amigo*," Sal said. "We're bound for heaven's gate, sentenced to death by this enormous saint." He murmured his last rites, "Have mercy, Lord, forgive us."

"Hey, Sal, who's the fatso in silk? Look how his robe stretches on his round belly," Blas said. He picked this time to regain his humor and called toward the fat man, "Hey, you, your dress is enough for my mother and my five sisters."

"Shhh, listen!" Sal said. How could things get much worse? A bell rang three times; a monk stepped forward.

"These men volunteer for service, *Excelencia Gàlvez*, your excellency," the monk said. He bowed to the fat man in silk.

"Who's the lard-ass *Gàlvez?*" Blas asked. Back to his old self, his words were funny, but irreverent and dangerous.

"*En el nombre del Padre*, in the name of the Father." The monk sprinkled holy water on their heads, "and the Son," he droned on, "and the Holy Spirit, amen."

"*Fíjate*, just imagine, Blas, we're blessed, not sentenced to death!" Sal inhaled new hope until he saw the truth of their predicament. They were forced from the jail and sentenced to servitude with the Spanish military. Soldiers hustled them toward the dock where they boarded a huge Spanish galleon. It was the same ship they had tried to steal food from.

"*¡Estùpidos!* Show some respect to our Royal Representative, Josè de Gàlvez, the King's Viceroy to New Spain," the soldiers said. The soldiers hit each passenger on the head and commanded them to bow as they passed the fat man.

"Did he say *Nueva España*, New Spain?" Blas asked. He stumbled on the gangplank. The gigantic ship swayed and creaked underfoot.

"Remember that story about the man who got swallowed by the whale?" Sal asked. He could feel the ship swallowing them, body and soul. He dreamed of taking exciting risks, but not this way. Was he dragging Blas into another nightmare?

CHAPTER 5

The Atlantic 1796

BODIES OVERBOARD

The prison crew, along with Sal and Blas, slept on the deck below the enlisted men, one deck above the pigs. All together, the Spanish galleon included six levels; ballast and cargo, livestock, prison workers, enlisted military, officers—and finally, the captain and his clergy guests. Sal and Blas drew the worst job on the ship. Many men were sick after breathing the livestock stench and sleeping in the cold dampness. As the weeks turned into months at sea, more than two dozen men became stiff and smelled of death. Sal and Blas were assigned to haul their corpses to the main deck and throw the bodies overboard.

"Just grab the poor bastard's ankles," Blas said. He needed Sal's help to drag a dead man to the main deck.

"We can use this man's extra blanket." Sal, still feeling guilty, was desperate to improve their situation. He slept huddled and cold every night with a constant rumble in his guts.

"You *loco*? I'd rather freeze," Blas said. He wrapped his hands in rags before he touched the dead bodies, then went back to work.

"Freeze if you want," Sal said. Blas was so particular about what he touched, ate, drank. Did he think he was on a cruise for his health? "If I don't get some sleep and something warm to eat, you'll be tossing me overboard soon." Once on the main deck, they waited for the Brothers to finish their prayers before they could pitch the poor fellows into the graveyard of the Atlantic. "You know what bothers me? Whenever I hear prayers for the dead, I think of the Brothers on the road to *Santiago*." Sal's stomach turned over when ravenous sharks approached the corpses. Each time he saw a body set adrift, his own fragile notions of God floated further away.

"Everything reminds you of *Santiago*. I'll never hear the end of it 'til the day I die," Blas said. "How many of the crew do you figure will become fish food in the next month?" He tossed his hand rags into the ocean, spat in his palms and rubbed them together.

"Okay, you're the one keeping track of bodies. Tell me this, have you noticed we only see the Brothers for last rites?" Sal said. "Where are they quartered?" Sal suspected the religious men on board enjoyed special comforts and privileges. If he fed his resentments, his fears shrunk.

"Near the Captain's quarters, I'll bet," Blas said. "They look clean and well-fed, not like the rest of us." Blas automatically made the sign of the cross on his forehead.

"And here they are always preaching about sacrifice and service," Sal said.

"*Deveras*, truthfully, I'd trade places with any of the Brothers if they'd give me a chance," Blas said.

"Yeah, keep dreaming," Sal said. He moved the conversation away from Blas's religious daydreams. Why even think of taking religious vows? It would get Blas into trouble one day.

The long voyage was prolonged with a supply stop at the island of *Hispanola*. The crew was quarantined on the ship and only allowed to hoist the new cargo and gaze longingly towards the docks that had some semblance of Spanish customs, foods and music. After a week in port, they were back at sea, entering a huge gulf. The men were as sick as ever, and more bodies were dragged up from the lower decks.

After delivering the bodies for burial-at-sea, Sal and Blas were ready for a rest. They scrambled back below deck. "Did you overhear Jimenez's story last night? What do you think?" Sal asked. While he lay awake shivering, he listened to petty officers like Jimenez and other enlisted men talk one deck above.

"All lies. I'm sure Jimenez is a drunkard; he's no Columbus," Blas said. He didn't trust the soldiers. They drank and told stories night after night. "I've told you, the only silver we will ever see is in our dreams." Blas knew Sal wanted to believe the tall tales of riches and fame in the New World. "Face it, we were tricked onto this rotten galleon. We're lucky we lived this long."

Sal thought Blas blamed him for their predicament. "But what if the stories are true?" Sal asked. Secretly, he still prayed for wealth for both of them. He grabbed the dead man's blanket and tried to sleep before the livestock in the hold began to make a ruckus.

"*¿Qué pasó?* What's going on down there?" Blas asked. He awoke when the deck below rumbled with extra activity. Something aroused the pigs and all their foul odors. "Those damn animals get fed more than we do."

Sal struggled to find a space between the deck slats to see the action. "Someone's moving the animals toward the ramp," Sal said.

"Get your sorry asses onto the launches, *pronto*," an officer shouted to the prison crew.

"Launches? We're landing?" Afraid the officer would use the whip on them, they heaved their exhausted bodies toward the shore launches, already loaded with livestock.

"*¡Adelante*, row!" the same soldier said. Sal and Blas leaned into the oars and pulled back, not expecting the overloaded craft to move an inch. The launch crept forward, then caught an unexpected sea swell and lifted toward a broad flat harbor. There were no docks, cliffs or watch towers like the port they left behind in *Cadiz*, Spain. This place appeared desolate.

"*¡Por Dios, vàmanos!* For God's sake, hurry up!" the Viceroy said. He barked orders from a fancy pontoon craft draped with flags, where he presided, fat and regal, as the first day they saw him in the prison yard.

"He doesn't miss any meals," Blas said. The

Viceroy's pontoon pulled past their launch. "The sea air must agree with him." The rowing was exhausting, but the fresh air reignited Sal's hopes for the New World.

CHAPTER 6

Vera Cruz, México
1796

JUNGLE

The Viceroy's pontoon reached the shore before everyone else. His military escorts lifted him by his chubby arms and feet, carrying him to the dry sand. Sal and Blas jumped in the shallows, then sloshed through the waves tugging their craft full of pigs toward the beach.

"¿Dónde estàmos, where are we? I'm sunk to my knees in sludge," Sal said. He and Blas herded the stinking animals off the landing craft.

"I can't tell the sticky mud from the pig shit," Blas said. Sand and sea swallowed their feet as they slogged across broad mudflats.

"It all stinks, brother," a nearby soldier said. "They call this place *Vera Cruz*—very cursed, we say." Soldiers shoved them forward as deep muck sucked at Sal's feet.

"God help us—these bugs," Sal said. The air carried swarms of pesky mosquitoes that rushed into his mouth each time he gasped for breath. "Is this *el Nuevo Mundo* or just some kind of purgatory?" Sal wondered. He grumbled as they scrambled for dry land. "First, the stinking jail, then the rotten ship, now another punishment from God." Layered with grime, Blas trailed behind. Even in the worst circumstances, he managed to surprise Sal with his idiotic behavior. Somehow, he mustered the energy to bellow an old ballad.

"This life full of sorrow..." Blas sang. Sal recognized the song, one they learned as boys begging for *pesos* outside the *cantina*. The disembarking soldiers also recognized the tune and joined in the singing. The Brothers moved toward shore, holding their skirts high after the landing party cleared the way. No one expected the Brothers to help herd the swine.

"*Gracias a Dios*, thank God," the Brothers said. Their prayers to celebrate deliverance from the sea voyage competed with Blas's barroom tunes. The soldiers kept singing along with Blas's bawdy songs, celebrating the landing with wine drizzled from *boda* bags held high.

"*¡Salud!*" the soldiers said. Sal watched as wine dripped into their open mouths. He licked his lips. Two of the uniformed men approached and offered Blas some wine. "*A nuestro trovador*, to the singer," one of the men said. He gave Blas a false salute. "*Señor*, your songs are too good for the pigs." The men ignored Sal. "This fellow will march alongside us. *Màs mùsica*, more music," they said. The soldiers encouraged Blas, the filthy fool, and offered him more wine in exchange for another song.

The Brothers were angered by the soldiers' interruptions of their holy chants. "*No más*, stop this at once," the Brothers said. The Holy men shuffled forward to restore order. Their religious robes sagged heavy with mud.

"Another song, Blas!" Sal said. He took advantage of the confusion since Blas made no move to grab the opportunity. "Sing 'The Lonely Widow.' Our audience demands it." He knew the soldiers would enjoy this lewd song and hoped it would offend the sanctimonious Brothers.

As Blas began the barroom ballad, the soldiers called out, "*Ustedes enfrente*, you men go to the front." Soldiers pushed Blas and Sal forward.

Blas relished his audience's response, pleased to get any positive attention. "I know we're in the same miserable predicament Sal, but it's our first promotion in the New World," Blas said.

"Just keep singing," Sal said. "At least we're ahead of the pigs."

Landing in *Vera Cruz, México*

CHAPTER 7

Vera Cruz, México
1797

EATEN ALIVE

The swarms of mosquitos in *Vera Cruz* were taking a toll on those who survived the sea voyage. The group of bedraggled travelers now faced a long treacherous march west to the capital of the Mexican territory known as New Spain.

"Get a move on," a soldier said.

"¿Y *por què*? Why bury them?" Sal asked. "These bodies will only rot in this jungle, like all of us." The deaths were so frequent their travel was delayed by weeks. Sal rolled the body of one of the Brothers into a shallow grave. For a moment, the dead man looked like Blas. Sal couldn't help himself from murmuring a prayer in secret. "Please let us survive," Sal said. Did he still believe God heard his prayers? No! "*Mira,*

Blas, these holy men die too," Sal said. "Where's their precious God now?" He knew Blas still believed in his religious training. How could he believe in a God who let so many men die? The ship lost half the crew since the day they set sail in *Cadiz*. Many of the men were already buried at sea. "These damned mosquitoes are making a meal of my body, and the fever gets worse each day," Sal said. Blas did his best, washing Sal's infected mosquito bites with his wine rations, something the Brothers taught him.

"If you had kept your mouth shut, we could have stayed in back with the pigs," Sal said. He wanted to blame someone for his misery. He targeted Blas. "We could have found a way to desert—get away from this mess. It's too late now," Sal said.

"Get away and do what?" Blas asked. "At least with the soldiers we get wine rations. If anything happens, the soldiers are here to protect us."

"What do you mean if anything happens?" Sal asked. He heard noises night after night but didn't want to admit his fears. "You haven't heard anything, have you?"

"Just be glad we're with the soldiers." Blas always tried to make the best of things. True enough, his singing did get them noticed. Now the singing only happened at night after an exhausting day. For weeks, they marched and cleared the jungle brush each day. By night they dug graves.

"The soldiers get machetes for this grueling work. Not us," Sal said. He always had something to complain about. One night, after digging graves, they settled in with the troops for food, wine and rest.

"Of course, they do. The machetes are for the *Tontos*," Blas said. They tried to get comfortable on the gravel mound. They were so tired it didn't matter after a while.

"The what? You do hear something at night, admit it," Sal said. What or who waited out there?

"I heard the soldiers talking about the natives—*Tontonacas*, *Tontos*—they call them. Sure, they're everywhere," Blas said. He knew Sal worried about everything. To cheer Sal up after many weeks on the road, Blas decided to add ridiculous stories to their routine—tales based on memories of their fathers' work as blacksmiths—including magical stories of enchanted swords and impenetrable shields. The soldiers loved it and it made Sal relax and smile.

"Thanks to your crazy new stories, the soldiers will believe we're magicians and blacksmiths. If only our fathers were here to laugh with us," Sal said. The evening songs earned Sal extra wine. It made him feel sentimental. While others dozed off, Sal began a new tune that only Blas heard.

"*Su Aminstad…*," Sal sang an old mournful song about loyal friends—a tune Blas recognized immediately. "Sharing our burdens through life, together…" Sal sang. He sang so sincerely, like an apology and a long overdue word of thanks for Blas's companionship. Sal would forget the incident, but Blas remembered it in the days ahead.

The western trek turned into months of hard labor—bushwhacking their own trail and disposing of the malaria victims. Finally, they arrived at the capital, *Ciudad de México*.

"*Oigan jòvenes,* you young men, get yourselves over here quick!" the soldier in charge said. The soldiers still spoke to them like they were kids. This one ordered Sal and Blas to follow other workmen toward the *Presidio*. The Spanish fort protected the settlement, housed the troops, stabled the best horses and stored all the weapons.

"*¡Blas, milàgro!* What a miracle! All this equipment," Sal said. Sal got a glimpse of the well-supplied fort. He felt like a real military man delivering more supplies. It gave him the opportunity to look over the whole settlement. "I've counted four workshops, a huge stable, an armory and barracks all around the fort." Sal's imagination filled with the possibilities of a good life here. "Imagine if we lived at this command post. Even the enlisted men get a bed and food. All they do is march around in fancy uniforms and intimidate *los indios.*"

Blas counted the horses and officers. "*Si deseos fueran caballos…*," Blas said. "If wishes were horses, beggars would ride." Blas had to listen to a new round of Sal's dreams for glory and wealth all day long.

The longer Sal worked among the soldiers at the Presidio, the greater his dreams of glory grew. His duties were simple, but being in the company of well-trained troops and crates of Spanish weapons and supplies made him feel important.

After three months of work in the *Presidio*, Sal and Blas were assigned to deliver a huge crate to the Mission compound, the second biggest organized settlement in the capital. Sal vowed, long ago, never to go near another church. "I'll go, but those Brothers better leave us alone," Sal said. He helped load tools and a crate onto an ox cart. Just another job, he thought.

"¡*Silencio!*" The Brothers warned the work crew as they entered the Mission grounds. Sal immediately reacted and made his complaints against the religious authorities.

"They wouldn't let us near this Mission church if they didn't need us to lug this rickety old cart," Sal said. "Damn these lazy Brothers."

"*Cuídate*, careful, Sal. They said, 'keep your mouth shut,'" Blas warned. His shoulders were slumped and his head hung low like some penitent sinner.

"They don't scare me," Sal said. He strutted forward in defiance of any restrictions.

"They should scare you. Look at the poor Indian over there," Blas said. The Indians hauled slabs of stone to build a wall surrounding the Mission. One poor fellow lagged behind the rest. Sal saw a rough wooden yoke restraining his legs.

"He won't last long. Think he's one of those *Tontos* you heard about? They'd never dare treat us Spaniards badly," Sal said. Why did he agree to come near the Mission? He wanted to return to the Presidio as soon as possible. At least the soldiers were real men.

"You two, put the cart near the base of the Mission tower," a Brother said. He ordered them to unload the wooden beams, ropes and rough-hewn planks. Sal and Blas helped other workers assemble a scaffold and a hoist for the cargo.

"*Bienvenido herrero*, welcome blacksmith," one of the other workers said. The well-fed fellow thrust a crowbar in Sal's hands. "Break it open," he said, motioning toward the remaining crate on their ox cart.

"Did he call you, 'blacksmith'?" Blas asked. Together, he and Sal tossed aside slats from the splintered crate. The daylight reflected off the cargo and made it shine.

"Look, Blas, it's pure silver!" Sal said. A Mission bell brought back memories of the riches Sal glimpsed in *Santiago*. The workers struggled to hoist the three-hundred-pound bell high above the ground. It became a holy moment for most of the men; the Brothers and many of the workers began to pray once the bell hung securely. "*Nuestro padre*, Our Father." Sal watched as the devout men got on their knees. Blas dropped to his knees too. He said, "Hail Mary, full of grace…"

"Pa-pardon me, sir," a man behind Sal tapped on his shoulder. The hefty man, the same man who called him 'blacksmith,' held out his hand to welcome Sal. "Th-thank you, sir," the man said. He sounded slow, kind of stupid, but he thanked Sal for delivering the bell.

"*De nada*, it's nothing," Sal said. He liked the attention, stood tall and responded as if he deserved all the credit. "I'm Salvador Tenorio, at your service," he said.

The big man stuttered, "Br-Brother David," the slow-speaking man said. Did this husky laborer call himself a Brother? "God has answered my prayers for blacksmiths." He gripped Sal's hand with bone-crushing strength. Blas jumped to his feet to make sure he took advantage of the man's prayers and got an introduction.

"Yes, we're truly blacksmiths, I'm Blas Bonilla," he fibbed. Sal was impressed with how convincingly Blas told this lie. He nudged Blas to make him aware of this man who spoke so slowly.

"*C-como yo*, as am I," Brother David said.

"Ga-glory to god! Two men to work for two whole years. I never thought my requests for more blacksmiths would be answered." This slow speaking man, Brother David, seemed to be a real blacksmith.

"Did he say two years?" Sal said. "What's going on here?"

"Come with me, I'd be happy to show you our humble shop," Brother David said. "God is truly gracious!" Sal did not want to tell the Brother that his prayers were not really answered, that he and Blas only pretended to be blacksmiths. He played along and took the tour.

"We'd be happy to take a tour before we return to the *Presidio*, Brother," Blas said. The three of them walked away from the other workers, still on their knees, mumbling prayers. They shared nervous glances with one another and trailed behind the big man, Brother David.

"I think there's been a mistake, Brother David," Sal said. Trapped by their own lies and clever stories, even a crazy man could tell they were imposters.

"D-don't you two worry, we'll w-work out all the paperwork when the V-Viceroy sends over your work orders," Brother David said.

His stuttering smoothed out as he began his tour. Aside from being a fool, this man had the Viceroy on his side. Sal and Blas hoped his flattery would continue, but they needed to fix the misunderstanding. How would Brother David react when they confessed that they were not truly blacksmiths, and they did not intend to stay at the Mission? Would he reveal them as liars? Before Sal and Blas could show any resistance to Brother David's plans, two men approached them near the Mission craft shops. One, a fat man, the other, only skin and bones. The skinny one dragged a shackle around his ankles. The fat fellow wore a frayed military decoration on his stooped shoulders— otherwise, he looked as shabby as his prisoner.

"Excuse me, Brother David," the short round man said. "These chains need work right away. This prisoner, Col. Diego Alvarez, can easily squirm his way free. He's still got thirty days left in confinement." The skinny prisoner, Diego Alvarez, pleaded with Brother David.

"Mercy, Brother David. *Por Dios*, I'm your countryman," the prisoner said.

"Shut your mouth!" The fat guard said. He yanked the chain attached to Alvarez's shackles.

"*Cálmate*, calm yourself, man," Brother David said. "God understands. He is with you in your suffering." He spoke in a patient, clear voice, first to the prisoner, then to his guard.

"You are in luck, we have two new black-smiths joining us today," Brother David said. He waved toward Sal and Blas. "Your repairs will be made soon." While Brother David talked to the guard, Sal leaned over to whisper to Blas.

"Looks like real trouble, Blas. This Brother David thinks we are staying here and the man in chains is a Spaniard. He's shackled and begging for mercy," Sal said. "Can you imagine his crime? We don't stand a chance unless we find a way out of this place quickly!" Sal and Blas did their best to look calm and innocent when Brother David turned to them.

"You see, so much work to do here," Brother David said. He continued to lead Sal and Blas across the Mission grounds and didn't seem to notice how they dragged their feet, as if they were already fitted with shackles. "We make tools and oversee the tanning process." He pointed out the tannery, the leather shop and a carpenter's shop. These shops were no more than shaded areas with rough benches, buckets and a few tools scattered on the ground. "We eat well." He patted his ample gut and pointed to the granary, a shallow pit with a grinding stone level with the ground. Next to it, an adobe oven shaped like a beehive. "Here, the bakery," he said.

"*Espera*, hold on a minute," Sal said. He stopped walking and breathed in the aroma from the bakery. He tried to remember the last time he smelled fresh bread or the scent of a woman. The bakery held both; maybe he could stay here for a short while.

"Oh, sorry, my Brothers. You're hungry, no?" Brother David said.

"Mmmmm, my mouth's watering," Sal said. Blas knew all of Sal's weaknesses and heard his true meaning. He shook his head, warning Sal away from his lust.

"Not here, not now. Don't get any ideas," Blas said. Brother David turned away to call out to someone in the bakery.

"*Prima* Gloria, bring us fresh bread," Brother David said. A girl, only eight or ten years old, walked out. Disappointed, Sal hoped to catch a glimpse of other women in the bakery. "*Gracias*, my precious." Brother David spoke gently to the little girl as Sal and Blas took the fresh, hot rolls she offered. "A beautiful child, *pobrecita*, poor thing. Her father is a Spanish soldier, her mother, a native: a half breed—*mestizo*—we call it." Gloria hurried back toward another woman who kept her distance. The sun burned directly overhead, and her tall, lean figure glowed with silver embellishments; bracelets, beads and earrings. The vision took Sal's breath away. Brother David noticed Sal's interest and pulled him away.

"Fresh *maiz*, corn," Blas said. "Look here, Sal." Anxious to distract Sal, he pointed out the workers shucking corn cobs and others grinding herbs, pulled fresh from the clay pots along the pathway. Sal continued to look back over his shoulder toward the bakery.

"Over here, the weavers, gardens and the vineyard," Brother David said. "Over there, see the well and the fountain." With a wink, Brother David made the sign of the cross on his chest. "And our winery!" Brother David said. He obviously wanted to impress his new blacksmiths.

"Sì, sì, God's gift to us, the grape," Blas said. He knew he sounded stupid as he tried to stall their arrival at the blacksmith's shop. Brother

David seemed a good sort, but sooner or later, they'd arrive at the forge, and the Brother would know Sal and Blas were not blacksmiths. They did not know an anvil from an anchor.

"God give us strength," Sal said. He also tried to stall, pretending to stumble. Maybe he could go back and rest at the bakery.

"Oh, careful!" Brother David said. "After your long journey, you need a little rest before you see our workshop. How thoughtless of me to think you'd start work right away."

"Brother David, a rest is a good idea before we return to the *Presidio*. But where?" Blas asked. How long would they be held at the Mission, and how long could they fool him?

"I prepared a place for you. Come," Brother David said. They followed him to a small adobe bunkhouse. Brother David leaned on the crooked door to open it. "So sorry, Diego left in a hurry. This door latch is broken." Inside they saw evidence of a struggle. A table tipped on its side with a broken leg next to an overturned chair. On the dirt floor, Sal saw deep grooves left by someone who had been dragged out.

"You mean Diego, the prisoner? Is this where you kept the criminal in chains?" Blas said.

"Oh, he's not really a criminal, he's only a poor workman who can't manage to tell the truth. He seeks a penitent heart for his lying tongue," Brother David said. "You two rest yourselves here while I go check on your orders from the Viceroy," Brother David said. "When you hear the bell, come out and join us for our first dinner together."

Brother David left them in the bunkhouse to think about their own lies and plot their next move. "When he discovers our lies, our dinner will be more like the last supper," Sal said.

CHAPTER 8

Ciudad de México, México 1798

CAPTIVE AT THE MISSION

After living so comfortably at the Presidio, Sal and Blas now found themselves captive at the Mission. It was over a year since their sea voyage had begun in Spain.

"Have we come all this way just to be controlled by the Church, again?" Sal said. They pretended to work and hardly realized that they were actually learning the Blacksmith trade with Brother David. They thought they learned a lot about the Brother, too. He was slightly older than the two of them, and he enjoyed the respect of all the other religious Brothers. He used his skills to create elaborate crucifixes, beautiful chalices and ornate silver work.

"*Que suerte*, we got lucky," Blas said. He

fumbled with the tools on the workbench in the Mission shop. "Can you imagine us making something used in the Mass?"

"Don't get too holy, *amigo*," Sal said. "Sure, Brother David seems like a good sort, for a religious man, but we are only staying here until I think of something better."

"Did you hear him say I have a gift for making candlesticks for the glory of God?" Blas said. He appeared very comfortable at the Mission, too comfortable. When Brother David left Sal and Blas alone in the Mission workshop, they shared their secrets.

"Okay, so we fooled him so far," Sal said. "But there is no way we are going to stay here for two years, Viceroy's orders or not." Sal wanted to get out and see other parts of this New World, especially the famous silver mines.

Relaxing after an evening meal, Brother David surprised Sal and Blas with a new proposal for their work. "I know you've traveled a great distance over the last year, but I wonder if you'd accompany me on trips to the countryside for deliveries and repairs at Mission outposts?" Brother David said. Sal wanted to hear more. It sounded like a good opportunity to explore and maybe even a way to regain his freedom.

"We find many souls to save outside the capital. There are so many good prospects for converts: the natives, the miners—all the folks we meet when we make deliveries throughout the country," Brother David said. He had begun to rely on Blas and Sal.

"Oh, yes, Brother. Let's make a trip right away," Sal said. He figured he'd use the trip to look for clues to the silver riches he spied among the natives. But the next week while Sal and Blas packed to travel with Brother David, Sal got nervous.

"I can see you are active to serve the Lord, Salvador. Good. We will prepare and leave for Puebla at the end of the year," Brother David said.

When the day of their departure to Puebla arrived, Sal began to worry about being stranded with the Brother. "If he starts some religious missionary talk, don't leave me alone with Brother David," Sal said. He could pretend to be a blacksmith, but he would never pretend to be a missionary.

"¿Por qué no? why not? He's a good fellow," Blas said. He always liked being around the Brothers.

"Too good. I feel nervous around him. You

talk to him about religious stuff while I look around," Sal said. "Just remember, some of these Brothers are rotten, like Santana," Sal said. They headed out to help load the blacksmith's wagon.

It took three days to reach their first delivery site, *Puebla*, from *Ciudad de México*. Valleys and hills made the going slow and boring. Their old wagon wobbled on the rocky pathways. Brother David told stories to keep them interested in the countryside. "Besides *La Catedral*, the town's got its own monastery, a library and a big central plaza. Seven tribes live in the surrounding valleys," Brother David said. "Some friendly natives work on the *rancho*s but beware of the natives who work the silver mines." This got Sal's attention.

Once they arrived, they found plenty of backbreaking work to be done. The outpost needed repairs, construction and many deliveries. Sal found it hard to sneak away on his own to look around, but he tried.

CHAPTER 9

Puebla, México 1799

SECRET SILVER

Blas and Brother David sat in the front of the wagon, chatting during a delivery to the grand *Catedral* near the marketplace. Blas kept his agreement with Sal; he took care of any religious talk with the Brother. After the delivery, Brother David left them to guard the wagon.

"Stay here like good little boys," Sal said. After Brother David hurried away, Sal mocked his instructions. "Who does he think he's talking to? Where did he disappear to this time?" No matter how fair Brother David seemed to be, Sal could not bring himself to trust him.

"*Otra vez*, once again, what's your complaint today?" Blas said. He secured the remaining cargo while he rolled his eyes and shook his head. "*Dios mío*. It's too hot. The road is too rough. The bell is too heavy." Blas could see Sal would never be content.

"¡*Despierta*, wake up, Blas! See this crowd, the vendors, the money," Sal said. He twisted around in his seat and pointed toward all the activity in the crowded market. "Why are we sitting here doing nothing?" Sal said. He poked his finger at Blas's chest, his patience running thin.

"The money, the silver, the women—all I ever hear is your big talk, ever since the pilgrimage to *Santiago*," Blas said. "It did you no good at all. Your poor mother."

"What have you ever done except follow me around?" Sal said. "I always protect you and figure out our plans." Sal peered into the crowd looking for opportunities for easy profits.

"Who would you kick around if not me?" Blas said. "I'm the one who got us on the galleon with the Franciscans." He eased toward the edge of the buckboard, ready for Sal's temper to flare. "I even got us jobs and our food," Blas said. "You're beginning to remind me of your dad, the drunkard." Sal threw a wild punch. Blas made a quick move to protect himself.

"*Cállate*, shut your mouth. Enough of this," Sal said. "Tell Brother David…," Sal said.

"Tell your own lies," Blas said. He held his ground. "Okay, you're the hero. *Bueno*, go ahead and find the silver."

"I found it already," Sal said. They both stopped to look into the crowd of shoppers. "See the *chica*, that girl over there?" Sal pointed to a young woman in the market with a basket of flowers on her head—her two silver earrings flashed in the sunlight. "Remember when Brother David told us to stay away from the Indians who work the silver mines, *¿y por qué*, why? He wants all this for himself," Sal said. He jumped off the wagon.

"You are shameless," Blas said. He grabbed for Sal's sleeve to hold him back. "You know, I would have done anything to go on a pilgrimage when we were boys. They say your Mamà took you to protect you from your father's drinking and womanizing."

Those words hurt Sal even though he thought all the pain had faded long ago. "And you're perfect?" Sal said. He struggled to get away, but Blas grabbed him. "You told lies to the soldiers about magical swords and shields. You lied about us being blacksmiths," Sal said.

"*Dios* gave me those stories," Blas said. They

wrestled under the wagon. "It got us in our blacksmith jobs with Brother David, didn't it?"

"God gave you the stories? You're as crazy as Brother David," Sal said. Did Blas really believe all this?

"Sure, *loco* enough to stick with you," Blas said. "Admit it; Brother David is the most kind-hearted man we've known. I'm not going to lie to him anymore. And I'm not going to cover for you." He called out as Sal disappeared into the crowd.

Girl in the Marketplace

CHAPTER 10

Puebla, México 1799
La Señorita Xichete

Sal followed the *chica* with silver earrings. He planned to snatch the earrings, but not while she had a crowd around her. Why did everyone want to be near her? Were these local vendors and native shoppers protecting her? She held her chin high, nodding to the right and left as she moved through the crowd. Seen as an outsider, Sal decided to stay a careful distance behind until she wandered to a more secluded place. He thought her colorful shawl would make her easy to track in the crowd. How had he lost sight of her? Did she cross over to the other side of the plaza? Two official-looking buildings stood on the opposite side of the plaza. Did she enter one of those doorways?

The first building held a broad entrance jammed with shabby peasants, waving their hands in the air as they argued with uniformed guards. The men in charge kept one hand pressed against the peasants' chests—holding them back, keeping them under control. This looked like the jail and the local police. Sal backed away from the place.

The second building looked like a postal station. The only activity consisted of three or four men bent over small writing tables like make-shift scribes. They listened to customers talk on and on. The writers scribbled on small squares of yellowed paper. Sal guessed the finished letters held few of the customer's actual words, yet the farmers, laborers, and even natives seemed well pleased with their documents. In any case, there were no silver earrings among these folks.

Behind the postal station, Sal spotted a narrow wooden stairway leading to a second-floor landing. It was a dim passageway. If the *chica* walked here, he could surprise her and snatch the earrings. As Sal drew near the stairway, he heard a man and a woman talking on the second level. To Sal's surprise, Brother David approached him from the top of the stairwell.

"Who's there?" Brother David said. "Ah, it

appears to be *El Señor* Salvador Tenorio. Are you playing explorer or spy today?" he said. The girl in the earrings peeked from the top of the landing. Sal got his first clear view of her face. Her brown skin glowed, smooth and beautiful. Her brows, raised in surprise, framed coal-black eyes. He noticed she no longer wore the colorful shawl.

"*¿Qué pasó?* What's going on here?" Sal said. He looked for an explanation, shocked to see Brother David and this lovely *chica* alone, together.

"I'll ask the questions," Brother David said. "Who guards the wagon while you chase young women?" He turned his gaze back to the *chica* at the top of the stairs. "Don't worry, I know this fellow, you're safe." He spoke to her as if he knew her well. Suspicious, but not knowing what went on between them, Sal acted the part of the Brother's obedient helper.

"I only came to tell you Blas feels ill. I'm looking for water," Sal said. Why did memories of Brother Santana race through his head? Dark corners, secret meetings, his heart raced.

"*¿Cierto,* truly? You searched for water all the way across the plaza?" Brother David said.

"What a loyal friend you are, Salvador. Why don't you come here and make yourself useful to me?" Brother David led the pretty native *chica* toward the dark corner room away from the stairs. He looked nervous and called back to Sal, "K-keep your mouth shut. Guard the door. Understand?"

Sal sat on a rickety bench just inside the doorway. Stacks of dusty books were piled high on the floor. As his eyes adjusted to the darkness, he strained to see what Brother David did with the *chica* in the corner of this stuffy little room. Could it be a school? There were no windows for light; shelves of papers cluttered the walls. Sal could see the girl's profile; her head bent low, she seemed to fumble with something, a sash, at her waist. He could see Brother David stood close enough to grab the loose end of her sash as she untied the binding. Sal's heart pounded.

"What are you doing to her?" Sal said. Just another rotten Brother, he suspected David all along. "You are a fraud. You are not a holy man." He had the proof.

"*Cálmate*, calm down Sal, no harm will come to her," Brother David said. He seemed amazingly secure for a man caught in such a sin. The girl clutched her arms over her chest. She held on to something. Sal leaped from the bench. He could help her escape like he helped Blas get away from Brother Santana years ago. He reached out to push Brother David away from her but she pressed herself toward the Brother as if she wanted his protection. "Allow me to introduce *La Señorita* Xichete, a true princess, the last of her tribe," Brother David said. He turned the girl toward Sal. Closer now, Sal saw a woman, not a girl. The most beautiful woman he ever saw. Brother David spoke in the same low voice he used for saying mass.

CHAPTER 11

Puebla, México 1799

Mysterious Codex

La Señorita looked like she would faint. Her face glistened with perspiration; she trembled, seemed feverish and most of all, afraid. "Get some cold water in a bucket, Sal," Brother David said. He held her arm and led *La Señorita* to the bench where Sal first sat. "Have no fear, trust God. Here, drink some water." *La Señorita Xichete* stared at Brother David. She clutched a stack of yellowed parchments in her arms. Before she let go of them, she bent to kiss the top sheet. Sal saw the papers ragged edges and symbols with crimson circles over black designs. "Take this medicine, please." He gave her a small envelope in exchange for her parchments. He took her gift and made a slight bow as if he were standing in front of his own Bishop and not some feverish native woman. "Go in peace, my daughter." He made the sign of the cross over her head. "You have done well. The greatness of your people will be remembered forever. Help her on the stairs, Sal."

La Señorita staggered just a little, held her hand against the shelves, then allowed Sal to guide her from the room, her silver earrings still dangling from her ears. At the bottom of the stairs, Sal watched her disappear into the crowd, then hurried back to Brother David, unsure of what he just witnessed.

"Why did you let her go? I thought you'd...," Sal said. His words burned in him. He felt like a foolish boy.

"I can only imagine what you thought, Sal. Life is often unkind, and any man is capable of acting like a fool," Brother David said. Sal eyed him with suspicion. He never told him about Brother Santana or his own Papá, yet David seemed to know his thoughts.

"God knows how easily we are tempted by our desires. For instance, even you followed *La Señorita Xichete* because of her silver earrings," Brother David said. "Let me show you some real treasures hidden in this little room."

Sal pretended to be interested in what the Brother said, but his mind fixed on *La Señorita* and her silver. How did Brother David know about being tempted by desires? Determined to protect her from Brother David, he hoped to see her again, alone. Meanwhile, Brother David said something about a library, waving his arms, referring to the stacks of books scattered around the room. Sal never saw a library in *Yuste* and did not care about Brother David's treasures.

"Are there any stories of risk and honor here?" Sal said. He tried to act interested until he could get away, find Blas, and tell him the truth about Brother David.

"Look at this special book," Brother David said. He acted innocent, as if nothing changed between them. He reached toward a row of worn leather bindings.

"*¡No más!* I'm done with your games," Sal said. He backed away from Brother David. "I'm not a boy impressed by your stupid secrets!" Angry and disappointed, he wanted to get out of the stuffy room.

"It's true. You are no child. This book proves you're a man, look here," Brother David said. He stood in Sal's way and held an open book in front of him. "They call this type of book a ship's log," Brother David said. He talked as if Sal were a child.

"Looks like something from the King," Sal said. He pointed to the golden seal at the top of the page.

"Yes, it's his royal mark in gold," Brother David said. "Here is a list of all the gold collected from your voyage." He pointed to a scribbled line. "And here, listed with the other men on the ship's crew is your own name, Salvador Tenorio." He paused to see Sal's reaction. Sal swallowed his feelings of anger toward Brother David and moved his finger over and over the line with his own name. "It's my job to protect all our records and accounts of our work here in New Spain." The Brother spoke, but Sal did not hear.

"Does this mark mean I am a real man of adventure? Will Papá ever see my name here?" Sal said. It must be a good thing to have your name in a book, one with the King's golden seal.

"*Fíjate*, just think of it, *Señor* Tenorio," Brother David said. "You are now a part of the history of your country." He gave Sal's shoulder a gentle nudge. "Listen, Sal, what happened in this room must be our secret. *La Señorita* is more important than you imagine. I did not meet her here to hurt her. Look what she brought me." He unwrapped the square packet of parchments. "She is the last of her tribe—her family—Salvador."

Could that be true? Sal wanted to help the mysterious *Señorita*. He wanted to know more about her. He tried to sort out all he'd seen. He could not read a word, but the thought of his name in the book burned in his mind. He knew the drawings on *La Señorita Xichete's* papers were not the King's Spanish, but what did they mean?

"These papers hold the secret records of her people," Brother David said. "You have to believe me." Brother David's hands trembled as he hid the parchments under his robe and hurried to lock the little library room. "Blas will wonder what's become of us. Lead us back to the wagon now."

They crossed the plaza where the morning market stood empty. Now the stalls were gone, but music and voices still filled the air. Evening customers filled the cantinas off the plaza. When Sal and Brother David reached the wagon, they found Blas asleep. He looked so peaceful Sal forgot all about their earlier argument.

"I've got to wake him and tell him what happened," Sal said. He savored the idea of having news to surprise Blas.

CHAPTER 12

Puebla, México 1799

SILVER EARRINGS

"Salvador, you swore you'd tell no one what happened with *La Señorita Xichete*," Brother David said. He reached for Sal's shoulder to hold him back.

"What about Blas? He won't believe what I saw. I've got to tell him," Sal said. He shrugged out of Brother David's reach.

"If you say anything, it could be dangerous for all of us," Brother David said. "I've shown you too much. The logbook, a tally of our gold collections, even *La Señorita Xichete's* tribal records. These are all secrets. Promise me, *secretos*." Why all the secrets? What did the Brother worry about? Sal reached out to wake Blas, who looked warm and comfortable in the wagon. Did he have a purple bruise on his cheek? Sal remembered the fight before he left the wagon. Only a few hours past, but it seemed like days. Everything changed.

"Please wait, I know you don't understand," Brother David said. "The Church fears all the native rituals and symbols. The soldiers are under orders to set fire to Indian altars."

"Then why are you keeping these things? Will you get in trouble?" Sal said. Why did Brother David do this bad thing?

"There's nothing to fear in these parchments or the symbols they hold," Brother David said. "I am afraid the Bishop will destroy the history of these people." He whispered to Sal, "I work with the Brothers who oppose the brutal treatment of the natives; we are here for their religious conversion." Sal didn't understand the Bishop's fear of the natives.

"Can we make sure *La Señorita* got back to her village safely?" Sal said. How could anyone think of *La Señorita Xichete* as a dangerous heathen? He wanted to see the fascinating young woman again.

"I promise, her village will be our first stop," Brother David said. "See the smoke curling above the hill? If we drive all night, we will be there by morning." He took the reins. Sal joined

Blas in back, to sleep as they traveled under a clear starry sky.

Brother David muttered to himself as he drove, "God forgive me, I feared for her life the f-first day I saw her." Just before dawn, Sal awoke. They were moving so slowly he decided to jump from the wagon and run ahead toward *La Señorita Xichete's* village.

"I'll get there faster and let her know you are coming," Sal said. Eager and full of energy, he hoped to see *La Señorita* right away.

"God's speed, Sal," Brother David said. "You may also see our novice, Cervantes. Tell him I am on my way." Brother David had driven the wagon all night. He drove so slowly; it took him an hour before the wagon came to a stop.

"*¿Dónde estàmos?* Where are we?" Blas said. He slept the entire way and finally awoke.

"We are stopping to visit my novice, Cervantes. He studies the local language in this native village," Brother David said. He looked toward the path and saw Cervantes, arm around Sal's shoulder, coming toward the wagon.

"What's wrong with Sal? Is he hurt?" Blas said.

Tears were streaming on Sal's face. "We are too late, too late," Sal said. "The fever took *La*

Señorita's life last night when she came home from the plaza. We lost her." Sal sobbed, confused and angry.

"Th-this is all my fault," Brother David said. He embraced Cervantes. "God forgive me," Blas looked from Brother David to Sal in a groggy haze.

"Why are we stopping here? To bury someone?" Blas said.

"Do not blame yourself, Brother," the novice Cervantes said. "*La Señorita* insisted on taking you those documents yesterday, even though she was very sick. Most of the tribe has already died from the diseases the soldiers gave them. We never know when they will come to take the native women away. The soldiers spread disease faster than we can spread the gospel." Cervantes held Brother David by the shoulders. "I've done as you asked, learned some of the symbols from *Xichete's* language. She trusted you, and now I will be able to interpret her parchments."

"She wanted her people to be remembered," Brother David said.

"Who is he talking about?" Blas said. Confused, he tried to get more information.

"Just help me with these shovels, Blas. You're right. We are here for a burial," Sal said. *La Señorita Xichete* needed to be buried. Sal could do this much for her. While Sal and Blas dug a grave, Brother David and Cervantes stood near the women preparing *La Señorita Xichete's* body for burial.

"The Bishop will punish us for our meetings with the native woman," Brother David said. "She struggled to keep the tribal rituals alive. We must respect her final wish."

One of the tribal women approached Cervantes with *La Señorita Xichete's* earrings in her hand. She motioned toward Brother David, and Cervantes explained, "They all know how she trusted you. You must take these." Brother David took the earrings and took a risk, offering prayers for her unsaved soul. Everything happened so fast. Sal felt guilty even though he did nothing wrong.

Blas worked quietly by Sal's side. He saw nothing special about this burial with Brother David taking charge. Why all the whispering and crying? "*¿Que es eso?* What are you doing now?" Blas said. "*¡Nunca*—never before!" He watched, astonished, as Sal kneeled while

Brother David offered prayers for *La Señorita Xichete's* eternal soul.

✳

CHAPTER 13

Ciudad de México, México 1799

BISHOP'S JUDGEMENT

After burying *La Señorita Xichete*, Brother David gave instructions to Cervantes, "Secure your notes about the tribal codex in our library, and thank you for your service." Sal, Blas and Brother David faced several days of travel on the road back to *Ciudad de México*. Their work now completed in *Puebla*; many new projects awaited them at the *Presidio*. Brother David remained silent; he handled the team of oxen and guided the wagon. Sal and Blas rode in the back of the wagon, recalling stories from their childhood.

"Mamà always said God protected me and wanted me to accomplish great things," Sal said. Trying to keep Blas distracted, he wanted to avoid questions about *La Señorita's* burial.

"Your mother must have known you needed her prayers," Blas said. He gazed at the clouds and twirled a long stem of grass in his mouth.

"It may be true," Sal said. He knew Blas referred to their rebellious boyhood days. Sal hid his worries from Blas, worries about Brother David's disobedience to the Bishop's rules. "Maybe Mamà guessed we would have this time in New Spain." He missed the simple days of boyhood. "Of course, we've only delivered supplies and discovered a few church secrets." He regretted his words the minute they left his mouth.

"What secrets?" Blas said. He didn't know the whole story. Now Sal's remark aroused his interest. Brother David overheard their conversation, too.

"Enough talk, you two. We've got to get some water for these oxen," Brother David said.

"Unyoke the animals and get them over to the stream." When Blas turned away, Brother David whispered to Sal. "*Cuídate*, be careful, Sal. Let's not drag Blas into our troubles." He had to caution Sal more than once.

After three days of travel, they spotted the

approach to the fort. Spanish troops had long ago established this command post. Brother David guided the wagon toward the stables of the *Presidio*. Sal and Blas expected to use the same bunkhouse and work in the forge. Brother David looked forward to rejoining the other Brothers in their daily routines.

Even before they were able to unhitch the oxen from their wagon, a messenger approached. He waived toward Brother David and held a rolled-up parchment in his hand. "You are required to report to the Bishop immediately," the messenger said. "Do not stop here. You must go directly to the Mission grounds."

"Now what?" Sal said. He and Blas were exhausted and filthy from the days on the road. Brother David said nothing. He only nodded to the messenger and took hold of the parchment, not even bothering to read it.

"We have our instructions. Don't take time to unload anything here," Brother David said.

"No time to eat? To bathe?" Blas said. He swiped his hands on his dirty sleeves.

Brother David gave Sal a quick glance. "The time has come, we've got to face the Bishop," he said. He flicked his leather strap on the oxen's back and gave Blas a weak smile.

"This could be a good time for one of your old songs, Blas," Brother David said. It took them an hour to cross to the Mission grounds. Not in the mood to sing, they rode in silence. Once inside the Mission grounds, Brother David put a plan into action.

"F-first, you two collect three deep bags from the weaver's shop," Brother David said. He counted out the steps of his plan on his fingers. "Then, get a small tooled b-box from the carpenters." As soon as they heard Brother David begin to stutter, Sal and Blas knew he felt nervous. Yet, he didn't seem to be surprised by this request from the Bishop. He already considered what to do. "Meet me back at our forge. Get the finest pieces of our metalwork and prepare them as gifts for the Bishop." It sounded to Sal like they were preparing bribes, not gifts, for the Bishop.

Blas, excited to see the Bishop, waved his hands as he talked. "Let's take the sundial, the silver goblet and a pair of candlesticks from our finishing table," he said. Blas worked fast, buffed, and polished each item then wrapped them in the cloth bags with great care. Sal noticed Brother David reach for the tooled wooden box and turn his back away. Blas kept wrapping and chattering.

"Your Mamà saw a vision," Blas said. "God has saved us for this work, Sal." He made the sign of the cross, as Brother David did so often.

"*Vamos a ver*, let's just see what happens," Sal said. "If you ask me, you and Brother David are both too religious. Just like Mamà." How could some people ignore the signs of danger until too late?

"The B-bishop waits for us, let us g-go," Brother David said. Each man clutched one of the bags as they crossed the Mission grounds. Sal remembered passing the Bishop's room only once, near a locked closet containing the holy vestments. He never expected to return. Now he lagged behind and dragged his feet on the crushed gravel pathway. He hated taking orders from anyone.

"We're heading for trouble, Blas," Sal said. "Brother David, is this Bishop more powerful than the Viceroy?" The only Bishop Sal ever saw presided at mass in *Santiago*.

"It isn't an e-earthy p-power, Salvador. G-god's spirit inspires his w-wisdom," Brother David said. Did he try to convince himself of the Bishop's wisdom? He could not control his nervous stutter.

Blas nearly skipped with excitement. "What do you mean, heading for trouble?" Blas said. "Tomorrow we'll pack for new deliveries, right Sal? I can't wait to see the Western provinces."

When Brother David stopped walking, he turned to face them. He needed to make the seriousness of this meeting clear to both Sal and Blas. He carried the smallest gift, the wooden box, out of sight, tucked under his robe near his chest. "Br-brothers, we will stand together before the B-bishop," Brother David said. Sal never heard David stutter so much. "I w-will present him with these g-gifts from our labors. I cannot be c-certain we will b-be allowed to d-depart together," Brother David said. Before they could ask any questions, Brother David turned away and entered the corridor leading to the Bishop's chamber. Wearing his plain grey robe, he walked past the vestment closet filled with silk shawls used only by the highest-ranking holy men. He nodded to the sentry guarding the door, and the three companions—Brother David, Sal and Blas—were allowed to enter.

"Your G-grace," Brother David said. He stood

before the Bishop, whose chair sat on a two-foot-high pedestal in the center of the room. A strip of deep blue carpet with golden emblems served as a boundary between the Bishop and the others. Behind his chair, an elaborate crucifix hung in the middle of the wall. Gold gilt frames featuring the Holy Father and Saint Francis hung on either side of the cross. Standing behind Brother David, Sal assessed the carpet, the pedestal and all the fancy objects looking so out of place in this outpost. Blas stared in awe of the Bishop until the man began to speak.

"You, Brother David, have been accused of being unfaithful in defending the Holy Church! Furthermore, you are accused of protecting the heathen and their sinful ways," the Bishop said. "Have you no respect for the memory of your own Franciscan Brothers, slaughtered by heathens in the north, in *Santa Fe?*" His severe condemnation fell on Brother David like a sudden storm. "It is my duty to remind you, these acts have put you in jeopardy of losing your own immortal soul." His stern gaze melted Brother David, the strong blacksmith.

"F-forgive me, Father, I've s-sinned. It's all

my d-doing," Brother David said. Sal's stomach clenched when he heard Brother David beg forgiveness in front of the Bishop.

"What's he talking about?" Blas said. His eyes darted between Sal and Brother David.

"It is the Lord's part to forgive and mine to bring you and your accomplices to repentance," the Bishop said. He turned his attention to Sal and Blas, one hand raised to his nose as if they were filthy vermin infesting his holy presence.

"You two criminals lied to get work as blacksmiths. You have taken advantage of the church's hospitality," the Bishop said. "You are unfaithful, not fit for service and have broken your baptismal vows with your disobedience." Blas swayed from one side to the other, squirming in the presence of this man who held them captive. Sal wanted to admit guilt. He knew the Bishop's accusations were right in his case.

"Allow me this s-small in-indulgence, your Grace, and we will depart from you," Brother David said. Maybe he kept a surprise in store to save them all. Brother David signaled Sal and Blas to hand the gift bags to an attendant who stood to the side of the room. The man looked like a rough henchman, a stark contrast to the silk-robed Bishop. The Bishop scorned the gifts held by his clumsy henchman. But his expression changed when Brother David took one step forward to present him with the small wooden box.

"And what's this?" the Bishop said. He did not lift his gaze from the gleaming silver gift inside the wooden box. When he finally spoke, he used a softer voice. "Brother David, we serve a merciful God. I have given your infractions deep consideration."

"You are wise and merciful, your Grace," Brother David said.

"Your sinful ways require a penitent heart. I have a good mind to send you north with our new Governador Diego de Vargas to restore the churches and order in *Nueva México*. But you are most fortunate. Just today Father Serra, our missionary Brother to *Alta California*, has informed me he requires more Brothers to accompany him," the Bishop said. "Prepare yourself. I have decided: you will be assigned to go with him. You will depart from this place, and from these men who have led you astray, immediately."

"It will be my honor," Brother David said. What he heard and witnessed shocked Sal. *La*

Señorita Xichete's precious earrings—wrapped in a little wooden box—paid for Brother David's freedom. How could Brother David truly be willing to be banished to an uncharted land with this man, Serra? So worried for Brother David, Sal barely heard the Bishop's orders to his henchman.

"Escort these two scoundrels to the *Presidio* brig to await their own sentencing," the Bishop said. He waved his hand to dismiss Sal and Blas. Brother David said nothing, but his eyes glistened with tears.

CHAPTER 14

Ciudad de México, México 1799

LEFT BEHIND

Soldiers came early to the brig in the *Presidio* to rouse Sal and Blas. "*Levántense*, get up, you've got work to do," a soldier said. He led them to the stables where they expected to see Brother David preparing for the new journey north with Father Serra. Over one hundred horses in ten corrals snorted and stomped, poking their noses in empty hay bins. Piles of manure steamed in the morning air. Wooden buckets with rope handles hung from the rails. The soldier in charge assigned Sal and Blas to feed, water and shovel one corral—ten horses—each.

"Something's wrong, Blas. Brother David didn't wait here for us before he went off with

Serra," Sal said. The animals eyed him, their ears twitching.

"Take this shovel and use it," the grubby corporal said. "You're not going anywhere, anytime soon. And no talking."

After three weeks of work in the stables, Sal and Blas lost all hope. "We shovel this damn barn, feed the animals; soldiers come and go all the time. No one feeds us half as good, and we're stuck here," Sal said. He complained, but it didn't change anything.

"At least we're together. Poor Brother David, all alone now, and where?" Blas seldom talked about Brother David anymore. He patted a pony between the eyes while he talked to Sal, never looking him straight in the face anymore.

"I don't know where he is, and I don't care," Sal said. He pitched a fork of hay in the corner of the stable and wondered for the one-hundredth time if he could boil some of the grass for extra food. They knew now that the Bishop had forced Brother David to leave them behind. But he didn't even send word to them. It hurt to think he never really cared. "We ought to think about how we'll get out of here," Sal said. He lost patience with Blas, who seemed resigned to talk to the horses all day. He had the nice animals to take care of; Sal's ten were mean and pushy. "I'm going to talk to the other stable hands tonight. At least they've got good stories to tell," Sal said. He now knew most of the men who worked the other pens. Their stories were mostly lies, the kind desperate men told to pass the time. But those *hombres* found a way to share a bottle every night and played poker, too. Sal even recognized the same bragger from their voyage to *Vera Cruz*, the man they called *Coronel* Jimenez.

"Come on and join us, Sal, we'll deal you in," Jimenez said. To his own surprise, Sal missed the companionship among the Brothers and blacksmiths at the Mission. He missed their work at the foundry, the hot food at the midday meal and the quiet, simple routines. After living among the good Brothers, Sal had to admit; he slipped back into a rough life with the soldiers. He played poker and drank himself into a stupor every night and tried to forget the life he lost. Why not? Blas kept to himself. Sal thought he could forget everything when he joined the other stable hands for a drink and a hand of poker.

"How long since we got paid? I'm not working for free," Jimenez said. Jimenez came from a family of businessmen. "We don't even get fresh food anymore," he complained to the others in the drinking circle. Sal agreed. During the weeks he spent here, there were no deliveries of fresh supplies to the *Presidio* from Spain or anywhere. "*Bueno*, here's a plan. We take these old tools and trade with the Pueblo Indians, maybe get ourselves a little fun in the meantime. By my calculation, the Viceroy owes us for all our labor, doesn't he? ¿*Y tú?* How about you, Sal, what do you think of my proposal?"

"*Bueno. ¿Como no?* Deal me in," Sal said. If no one else was going to take care of him, he might as well turn to a life of crime. This fellow Jimenez had an idea.

"It won't be the first time a squaw gets traded for a shovel," Jimenez said. The men responded with laughter and snorts, shifting their pants in anticipation of female company. Sal heard the crude words. "Trade for a squaw," Jimenez had said. He thought of *La Señorita Xichete's* beautiful face. Why did he keep company with these men?

Remembering his real friend, Brother David, he felt guilty and tried to change the subject away from stealing tools and trading for squaws.

"What's the news from the troops with Serra? Any word?" Sal said.

CHAPTER 15

Ciudad de México, México 1800

OPPORTUNITY

Every night the poker players spewed new complaints. Sal was bored with their whining. He came to expect more talk than action. Jimenez was different, a show-off, he was always the leader. "I'm sick of this rot-gut *pulque*," Jimenez said. The fort's wine and rum from *Hispañola* ran low, all of it now reserved for the officers who spoke of nothing but the anticipated arrival of some important church leader. The stable hands were limited to the rumors of the visitor and the rough liquor they got in trade with the local natives.

"How much you want to bet I can hijack the officers' wine while they are busy gossiping about the important visitor?" Sal said. He challenged

Jimenez and spoke before he thought through his scheme.

"I'll bet my *pistola*. You will get *nada*, nothing," Jimenez said. He was a blowhard, always game for a wager. Now Sal had to follow through on his bragging. It was months before he finally figured out a way to steal the officers' liquor. He knew they ate in a special dining room with visiting dignitaries. Finally, the visitor arrived. The low glow of the lanterns signaled the special dinner and liquor close at hand. Sal found his way from the barn, across the *Presidio* compound, to the officers' dining room. He hid outside, crouching below the dining room window sill, listening to the men's conversation from his place in the shadows. One angry voice rose above the others. Sal tried to make out who spoke.

"I have not traveled for months and come all the way to return to my men empty-handed," the angry man said. "I do the work of God Almighty, gentlemen!" This voice boomed out from the officers' dining room. "*El Rey*, the King, established our well-being, our supplies as his highest priority!" This cleric spoke in a tone Sal never heard before. The man didn't hesitate to press his demands on the highest military officers.

"The Missions already receive everything possible, Father Serra. Don't doubt our faithfulness. It's the King who cut our supplies," the Captain of the *Presidio* said. The name, Serra, rang in Sal's ears. The same missionary the Bishop ordered Brother David to follow. "*Por favòr* Father Serra, your demands are too great." The military officer responded with such caution; it surprised Sal.

"*Por Dios*, by God, I expect a dispatch of new supplies from this *Presidio* immediately. Prepare a new detail of your most able soldiers to accompany me at dawn," Father Serra said. Sal swore he'd join the detail in the morning. What an unexpected stroke of luck! Finally, good news to share after months of hard work and estrangement from Blas. Sal forgot all about getting any liquor from the officers and went immediately to look for Blas.

"Where the hell are you?" Sal said. He'd gone directly to their sleeping quarters outside the stables. The two of them hadn't talked much over many months because Blas disapproved of Sal's drinking friends. This good news would bring them back together. "Hey Blas, you'll like this. A real missionary—it's the Serra fellow." Sal's words fell into empty space. Blas's absence ruined the good news. What if Blas abandoned him too? Sal dropped to his knees, "*¿Dónde esta, Blas, God, where?*" Sal cried out, desperate to see his old friend, "First Brother David, now Blas is gone, why make everything hard for me?"

God answered. "I hear your prayer, my son," the hem of a grey cassock brushed against Sal's arm. His body shook with fear. "Salvador, your sins have cast you into despair." A Brother came out of nowhere and offered Sal a jug of water. Sal thought he recognized the voice, but not the man who spoke. "The Lord spoke to me, my son." Now Sal recognized Blas's familiar grin.

"You fool! You scared me!" Sal said. He knocked the water jug out of Blas's hand.

"Careful, can't you take a joke?" Blas said.

"What are you doing in the robe?" Sal said. "This is serious."

"What? You won at poker?" Blas said. He had lost faith in Sal's friendship, but he had his own news to share. "*Escúchame*, just listen to me. I arranged everything. At dawn, we'll travel with Father Serra. Because of my clever work, while you were off playing poker, we have a chance to find Brother David in *Alta California*." Without knowing it, he stole the good news away from Sal.

"How'd you know all this? And what's with the robe?" Sal said. He wanted to be the one to save the day.

"This robe got me assigned to recruit Serra's workers," Blas said. "It's not an easy job. No one wants to go to *Alta California*. Do you volunteer, my son?" Blas knew his religious tone annoyed Sal.

"Of course, I volunteer, you fool," Sal said. "Why are you dressed in the robe?"

"While you were wasting day after day with the stable hands," Blas said, "I kept warm in the *Presidio* chapel. The poor old Brother assigned to the chapel never gets any visitors. He wanted to escape before Serra arrived and dragged him north, so he gave me this cassock and left me in charge."

"Ha, you should thank me for pushing you toward the chapel," Sal said. He wanted to take credit for something. "*Bueno*, Brother, I volunteer. And let's take that man, Jimenez, too. Believe me; he could be useful."

"What do you mean, 'useful'?" Blas said. "Isn't

he one of the drunkards who plays poker in the stable?" Blas hated the men who turned Sal back to his old ways.

"Trust me. I'll go find him now," Sal said. How many times before had he asked Blas to trust him? This time they were going to be freed from the stables, from the *Presidio* and the Bishop's punishments.

The poker game had ended by the time Sal made it back to the barn. The winnings were piled in front of Jimenez, as usual. "*No más*," the other players said. They trailed away from the game one by one.

"*Otra, otra*, again," Jimenez said. His words slurred. Sal helped him back to his barracks, hoping the night air would sober him up.

"*Fíjate*, just imagine; new territory, *Alta California*," Sal said. "We could head out in the morning. You see how your pay and your supplies are dwindling," he said. "The church has money to support us, and we can get away from Serra as soon as we want."

"Desert the post?" Jimenez said. He could not see the opportunity. Sal made it clear.

"A reassignment, *Coronel* Jimenez. An exploration of the wilderness, land, glory. This could expand the Jimenez family business," Sal said, "Let's pack your things."

At dawn, Sal, Blas and Jimenez loaded cargo for Father Serra in preparation for the expedition. Blas, still dressed in the Brother's grey robe, Jimenez barely awake and Sal rethinking his hasty decision.

"Lord, give me patience." Father Serra looked toward the clouds. "You men must follow my instructions," he said. "Everything's wrong. Listen, when I tell you the corn gets packed dry—the oil, well-sealed." Father Serra acted more demanding than any officer in the military. "And another thing, we'll need twice as many chickens. You, go collect them at once." Father Serra shoved Sal's shoulder. He kept rechecking his inventory list of supplies.

"We're ready now. Let's get moving," Sal said. He wanted to begin the search for Brother David. He counted and recounted all the food, the tools, timbers—everything.

"Who's in charge here?" Father Serra said. He scribbled in his books. "We're ready when I say we're ready. *¿Sabes, hermano,* you understand?" Father Serra turned to Blas. "What's your name?"

"Brother Bonilla, Father. The man means no

harm," Blas said. He covered for Sal. Blas looked like a real friar in his borrowed cassock. "Here are, *Coronel* Jimenez, also Salvador Tenorio, at your service," Blas said. Father Serra added the names to his official ledger. Now their lives were in his hands.

CHAPTER 16

Sonora Desert, México 1801

A Broken Axle

Jimenez suffered from his hangover for two days trailing behind Father Serra. He belched and groaned like a man who spent over a year playing poker and drinking. Even though he claimed to have a wealthy family in Spain, they would never recognize their son—unshaven, unwashed, trudging through the desert. "*Míralo*, look at him, I've never seen a padre move so fast," Jimenez said. Even in his grubby condition, Jimenez's keen eye never missed a thing. "Serra's got a limp, but he's quick and so focused on keeping those stupid lists of kilometers traveled, the weather, supplies, converts. We are lucky Brother Bonilla manages to keep pace with him."

"I just hope Blas is smart enough to get some information from Serra about our friend Brother David," Sal said. "*Màs ràpido*, Jimenez, let's go faster. We can't lose them," Sal said. By sundown, Father Serra and Blas walked miles ahead of Sal and Jimenez. They struggled to haul the over-burdened supply wagon through the sandy soil. "Put your shoulder into it," Sal said. Rocks and ruts made the pathway uneven, at times, impassable. "It's going to take us two days to catch up with them at this rate."

On the third day, Father Serra finally slowed his pace. He discovered a small band of natives to baptize. "*Gracias a Dios*, the baptisms stopped him," Sal said. He and Jimenez stood apart and watched Father Serra preparing for the impromptu ceremony.

"We must get their names in my tally of baptisms," Father Serra said. "Brother Blas: do your part, get the holy water." Blas flicked holy water with his pudgy fingers onto the surprised natives. So clumsy, half of the blessed *agua* dripped along his sleeves.

"Look at those natives: dirt poor, but they still offer Father Serra gifts," Sal said. Jimenez and Sal hid as they watched the spectacle. Blas nodded and muttered, doing his best to perform the ceremony.

"They'd be better off if we gave them a few supplies, not just holy water," Jimenez said. Sal liked his blunt honesty. The son of a rich man, Jimenez spoke his mind. The new converts loaded them with offerings. Sal figured out how to pile the baskets, blankets and stone carvings into the overcrowded wagon. The load proved too much for the wagon. It wobbled for a few feet, then made a loud cracking sound and the wheel gave way. The cart tilted to one side and spilled over on the ground.

"What in the name of God did you do now?" Father Serra said. His temper spilled over, too. "*Ay Dios*, you know I'm faithful, why do you test my limits?" He shook his fist toward the sky then turned his angry mood on the men. There was no way for Sal to cast blame on the gifts loaded on them by the neophytes. He stood back to see what would happen next.

Serra spun around to face them, his face red with fury. "You men fix this." He grabbed a blanket, dried meat and a water jug from the broken cart. "Get out of the way." He pushed Sal back. Sal stumbled backward, amazed by the temper wrapped within Serra's holy robes. "The work of the Lord cannot wait." Loaded like a pack mule, Father Serra told Blas to do the same. "Get what you'll need to make camp, Brother Bonilla, it's a long walk."

Blas's hands shook as he pulled a canteen from the heap of supplies, a small spade and a length of rope.

"*Coraje*, courage," Sal helped tie the load of supplies on his back.

"You stay safe, Sal. Meet us as soon as you can," Blas said. He did not want to go on alone with Father Serra. He worried, was this God's punishment for imitating a holy man? Sal was having the opposite thought.

"You have my promise—I will find you." Sal tried to encourage Blas. Now he could see that the robe suited Blas, who had always wanted to be a cleric.

"We'll go ahead: you two stay, repair this wagon," Father Serra said. "Whatever happens, guard the rest of the supplies and meet us at the coast."

CHAPTER 17

Sonora Desert, México 1801

THE UNIFORM

The broken axle delayed everything. Sal could use his lessons from the foundry with Brother David to do the repair. "As a laborer, you are useless, Jimenez," Sal said. The son of a rich man never learned about welding a broken axle. Sal realized it would be easy to abandon the damned supplies, but he could not abandon his promise to Blas. "Just keep the fire going. *Digame*, tell me one of your stories." Ever since he met Jimenez, Sal knew he liked to tell stories and brag about his family's business in Spain. Sal heated a crude mallet to pound the wagon's cracked axle. "This is going to take all night," Sal said.

"Did I tell you how *mi abuelo*, my grandpa,

arranged everything? He fixed it for me to join the military as an officer," Jimenez said. Sal heard this story before. "He wanted me in this *Nuevo Mundo*, a chance to get the family some free land," Jimenez said.

"Your own grandfather put you here just to make your family even richer?" Sal said. It reminded him of how his own Papá tried to use him and Blas to work for him. "Just think of your family, a long way from you now," Sal said. He bent near Jimenez, clutching the red-hot axle. Sal could not help but notice how close to his own age, height and weight Jimenez appeared. "So much influence, and there's nothing they can do to help us." He envied Jimenez. They also shared the same color skin, eyes and hair. "Y *ahora*, and now it's just you and me." His imagination worked overtime. Now that they were outside the control of the *Presidio*, what if Sal could somehow trade places with a guy like this?

"Can we get some sleep? It's been a long day," Jimenez said. He pushed the sandy soil into mounds and unrolled two thick blankets from his bedroll. Sal watched him from the corner of his eye. "Here, this one is for you." He laid under one blanket and tossed the other toward

Sal. Jimenez relaxed as if he didn't have a care in the world.

The Devil taunted Sal during a sleepless night. He heard the breeze fluttering in the bushes, but then, he clearly heard someone speak his darkest thoughts. "How much easier do you want me to make it for you?" the Devil said. "This man sleeps right here next to you. Use the mallet, finish him off; take his identity and start a new life."

"It's too easy. It would never work," Sal said. He tried to imagine how Brother David would advise him. He would be proud of how Sal fixed the wagon, but ashamed of his murderous thoughts about Jimenez.

"You idiot! If you don't listen to me, there will be no second chance," the Devil said. He sounded like a bully trying to frighten a boy.

"I'm not so sure I want to listen to you anymore. I can handle this myself," Sal said. He spoke out loud in anger, wrestling with his demon.

"Handle what?" Jimenez said. His groggy words startled Sal.

"This axle. I handled the axle. It ought to be alright now," Sal said. As the dawn broke, he resisted the Devil and stood, proud of his repair work.

"You fixed the wagon?" Jimenez said. There was a note of surprise and admiration in his voice. Sal took it as a compliment. He would continue the journey for Blas's sake. He needed to take charge and let the Devil, and Jimenez, know it.

"You can read a map, right, Jimenez?" Sal handed over the crumpled parchment Father Serra left to guide them to the coast.

"I'm not useless at everything. I know how to find my way," Jimenez said. He took Serra's map, jammed it in his pocket and started a new story as he rolled his blanket. "You think I've got it easy, right?" Jimenez said. "A wealthy family is harder to live with than you think. I can't afford to make a mistake or fail in the New World." He pointed toward the horizon and kept on with his story. "Look, we head westward," Jimenez said. "See where Serra marked the river? *Rio de las Cañas*, says here." He refolded the map and kept talking. "My father always tried to impress my grandpa." Jimenez walked ahead of Sal lost in his memories and his story. "Papá saw what happened to his younger brother, *Tio* DD," Jimenez said. "*Que làstima*, so sad. Born an idiot, a stutterer." With the assurance of an Indian guide, Jimenez pointed to markers in the landscape. "Look, see where the cactus stops and leafy plants grow? Those acacia trees mean there's water nearby."

"*¿Como un indio*, are you part native? How do you know all this?" Sal said. The plants and dirt and rocks were all one dreary blur to him. Just when he thought he knew all about Jimenez, he heard some new story. Intrigued, Sal asked, "So, what happened to your uncle, *Tio* DD?"

"Grandpa, so embarrassed by his idiot son, kept him hidden from everyone. Papá called him DD because he couldn't even say his own name, David," Jimenez said. He focused on the map. "Look, we're heading to the river. Papá taught me to scout the markets near the rivers. He'd say, 'it's where the villages start, *mijo, el rìo.*' Those rivers lead to the ocean—it's where we meet Serra, *¿sì?*" Jimenez tried to help out. Near the river, they did begin to hear voices and they spotted some dogs and chickens.

"I guess your Papá knew his business," Sal said. He wondered if Jimenez missed his father. A man can miss even a cruel, demanding father.

Small *pueblos* began to appear. Little round huts, women dipping water gourds in the river and native men chipping away at tender sapling branches with flint rocks.

"This is what we do at home. We find new markets," Jimenez said. He didn't waste any time approaching the men with tools to trade for food. Jimenez traded some of the church's cargo in each village they passed through for the next seven days. The natives gave the few things they owned in exchange for the church goods. Some offered rough *pulque* liquor in exchange for their goods. One native man (who seemed to be drunk on his own *pulque*) even offered to trade his daughter, a skinny pregnant girl who held her belly like a water jug.

"Do you think this is one of their customs?" Jimenez said. Sal blushed, embarrassed by the gesture. The memory of *La Señorita Xichete* came back to Sal. He resolved that he would never act like the other soldiers, abusive toward the native women.

"Want to trade for her?" Jimenez said. "Some things are better than *más dinero, amigo.* Let's give her a try." He walked around the girl giving her a close look from all angles. She kept her

eyes cast downward, embarrassed for herself—
or maybe, for her drunken father.

"The military uniform charms the girl," Sal
said. "Do you think the jacket would fit me?"
Only half-joking, Sal kept talking, hoping to
distract Jimenez.

"This jacket is dirty and torn, but it still has
its benefits," Jimenez said. He kept his eyes on
the woman and didn't seem to notice how interested Sal became with his satchel, his *pistola*
and all his military issued gear.

"Let's take the food and leave the girl," Sal
said. His conscience would not let him consider
the native women as payment for the church
goods. His envy of Jimenez's few possessions
kept gnawing at him. "So, whatever happened to
your *Tio* DD?" Sal said. He kept Jimenez talking.

"Finally, my grandpa paid off the Brothers at
the church to take DD as a servant, and my Papá
never saw his little brother again," Jimenez said.
"It's my family, Sal. You see why I cannot fail."
Sal thought of the story all day.

At night they camped at the river. They
worked their way along the riverbank for a
second week: their goal, the Pacific coast. But
Jimenez walked slower each day. He coughed

between every word he spoke, and his storytelling slowed down. Near the port city of *Mazatlán*, Jimenez's skin began to look grey and splotchy. He choked on most of what he ate. Too tired to stay on his feet, he slept more than half the day. At night he rolled on his blanket, fighting a fever.

"We'd better lay off the *pulque*," Sal said. He needed to complete this trip with Jimenez as a partner. Chances were better of reconnecting with Blas and Father Serra if they worked together. Just outside *Mazatlán* they met other travelers who looked like a bunch of cutthroats. Sal worried about their safety. "Do you think some of these men are *banditos*?" Sal said. "What if they attack us for the church goods?" Jimenez, who had been silent for days, gave no response. Sal, the healthy strong one, felt pressure to protect the remaining goods, tend to Jimenez and keep an eye out for Blas. "*Descansa* Jimenez, lay here awhile." Sal found a hillside space protected by a few shade trees. Breaking off low hanging branches from a scrawny pine, he camouflaged the cart.

"Do you know the *Nuestro Padre*, the Our Father?" Jimenez said. His faint request surprised

Sal. Did he ask Sal to say the Lord's Prayer as his last rites?

"Just rest Jimenez," Sal said. He patted his shoulder and tried to encourage him, but Jimenez looked bad. "*Duermes*, you sleep now and dream of the ocean." They were so close to the Pacific; if Jimenez slept off his fever, they'd make it to the coast together. Sal didn't want him to die.

The next morning Sal awoke early. As long as he and Jimenez were camped out-of-doors, they were vulnerable to thieves. They still had a few church goods to protect. "I'm going to uncover the wagon and get ready to head into town. We are so close," Sal said. "Come on, this could be the day we find Blas and Father Serra." He nudged Jimenez with his toe and watched to see him move. Nothing. "You can't sleep here all day," Sal said. He bent to push on Jimenez's shoulder and felt his body—cold, stiff, unresponsive.

"Not this, God! Not so close to the ocean," Sal said. He shook Jimenez by his shoulders. Not a deep sleep, but the same death Sal witnessed over and over among the sailors on the Atlantic crossing. "I did not kill him when I could, Lord.

Now you take him from me?" Sal remembered all the graves he dug outside *Vera Cruz* for the malaria victims. Now he needed to dig another grave, for Jimenez.

"Damn, damn, damn you, little rich boy," Sal said. He muttered to himself as he pulled a shovel from the cart. Sal dug a shallow grave and buried Jimenez beneath one of the shade trees. What killed him: the mosquitoes, the *pulque*? Would sickness or death await Sal too?

Struggling to remember the Our Father prayer, Sal dropped the shovel. Jimenez deserved some kind of last rites, but Sal felt too mad to pray. Mad at Jimenez for dying, mad at Blas for leaving him behind and especially mad at God for making him struggle. "Sleep well, Jimenez, dream of the ocean," Sal said. He left the cart under the bushes, planning to come back for it after he found Blas and Father Serra at the coast. If he found them. He lifted Jimenez's uniform jacket and slung his military satchel over his shoulder. A few days ago, he considered killing Jimenez for these grubby rags. Now they were the only things his friend left behind. He began his walk in the direction of the salty ocean breeze.

By early afternoon Sal entered the port town of *Mazatlán*. The uniform worked well to attract attention and respect. "*Salùdos Coronel*," a stranger said. The man stood straight and eyed Sal with wary respect. "*Pase usted*, come this way." More dock workers stood aside to let Sal pass. He used Jimenez's papers as his own identification. Not used to this treatment at first, he soon became comfortable hearing people call him by Jimenez's name and rank. Sal walked the docks asking questions. No one seemed to know anything about the two Brothers, Serra and Blas.

"You there, which of these vessels go north?" Sal said.

A barefoot dock worker, a burly man with scarred arms stepped forward. "*Coronel*, every week many leave for the north, *Alta Califòrnia*. *¿Sabes?* Understand?"

CHAPTER 18

Mazatlán, México
1801

THE DOCK GIRL

A working girl on the docks of Mazatlán balanced a tray on her hip. "*Cerveza*, cold drinks, beer!" Rosa said. The voice of this small, delicate woman boomed above the other vendors. The red silk shawl draped over her shoulders gave her a devilish look. She and the other women on the dock sold more than cool drinks. "Good business, many ships, many men." Her business began with a cunning welcome and a promise to show Sal around. "I show you port, *Coronel*. Want drink? Want Rosa?" She stood by his side as he assessed the passengers loading for northern ports. He did not intend to buy her beer or her time. *Mazatlán* hosted a lot of traffic: freighters, fishing boats, and even a ship with a French flag like those Sal remembered at the harbor in *Cadiz*. He counted the flags of many nations on ships of different shapes and sizes. The possibilities to set sail and investigate were endless. "¿*Si, o no, soldado*? You got something for me in your bag?" How could someone so small be so intimidating? She waved her shawl and pointed to Jimenez's satchel slung over Sal's shoulder. He protected his twenty *pesos*. "You tired, you come rest with Rosa." She took hold of his arm.

Before Sal thought about it, they arrived at her tiny room. Rosa caressed an embroidered silk pillow and urged Sal onto the bed with no intention of resting. An experienced sorceress, she reached into his satchel, extracted two *pesos* and made them disappear into a fine ceramic vase. "*Mira*, silk *de China, soldado*, Chinese silk," Rosa said. Without her shawl, he could see her boney little shoulders, proud and pathetic at the same time. She lifted her plain dress, underneath she wore a blue silk camisole—a previous customer's gift, no doubt. She curled up next to Sal.

Rosa loved to talk, her voice alternating between bold and rough to girlish. She recalled a list of previous clients for Sal. "Big men,

Russians; stink like seal hides. The French men; skinny, smell of sandalwood." Sounding like a harbormaster, her list of ships and sailors continued. "Y *los* Yankees, bad for business; *nunca*, stay one night." Rosa kept close track of her time and money. She frowned and wagged a finger of warning, "*cuídate los Portuguese, con mucho oro y negros, todos peligrosos*, too dangerous. I no go with *Portuguese*," Rosa said.

Sal wondered, is she serious or crazy? Angel or Devil? He did know she took two of his precious *pesos*, and he needed to use his remaining eighteen *pesos* to search for Blas and Father Serra. She finished her warnings, grabbed her vase with one hand and gave Sal a child's salute with the other. "*Mi Coronel*," she said. She started on her way toward the dock to look for new clients.

Alone in the quiet of Rosa's room, Sal inspected Jimenez's satchel. He could not read the official papers or even a handwritten note, maybe from Jimenez's father. When he unfolded the note, a few *pesos* fell from the envelope. Sal said a silent thanks to Jimenez's Papá and tucked the money out of sight. Ah, back to twenty *pesos* in the satchel, again.

Over the next few days, Sal walked alone on the docks. Rosa disappeared, but no matter, he reminded himself of his goal to find Blas and Father Serra. One morning he heard a familiar song, one of Blas's favorites, sung by a drunken sailor. "Quite a song, *hombre.*" Sal patted the ruddy-faced man on the back to get his attention. "Is the song from your country?" Sal said.

"No, no *Coronel*, it's a gift from a little friar," the singer said. He described a short, chubby religious cleric who had taught him the tune. Had this man met Blas?

"I'd give my confession to such a cleric. Where can I find him?" Sal said.

"Not here, he and the other religious man sailed two weeks ago to *San Diego* on a fine new clipper," the singer said. Sal knew his next destination needed to be *San Diego*. A scheme to book passage formed in his mind, and he needed Rosa's help. With twenty *pesos* left to pay for her services, Sal hunted for the dock girl.

"*Hay, ¿Rosa La Totorame? No, no, no,*" the dockworkers said. Sal learned not to ask for her when his first inquiries were met with winks and waging fingers. He guessed she used her tribal name, *Toto* or *Tonto*, or some native band in this region. Scouting the ramps, he stepped beyond crates and over coiled ropes, then caught a glimpse of her red shawl. Yards from where a French ship docked, Rosa's shivering body lay on the damp planks, curled under her shawl.

"Rosa, you hurt?" Sal said. Why did he feel so urgent over such a woman? Perhaps, just because he needed her help.

"*Coronel*?" Rosa said. A kitten would mew with a louder voice. Her shawl covered her bruised face, dry blood caked under her nose. Sal bent to lift her frail body.

"I'll take you. Your Mamà? Papá?" he said. She shook her head with a vacant expression on her face. He wanted to take her home but remembered her shabby room seemed no more than a converted shipping crate. "I'll take you to rest, get you some water," Sal said. Rosa's lips opened with tiny gasps.

"I meet bad man," Rosa said. Sal carried her to a rented room with a bath. After two days of care, food and water, and ten whole *pesos*, Rosa's color returned.

"Can I trust you? I need a special favor," Sal said. Though he saved her life, it embarrassed him to be one more man asking something of her. "Can you help me? Do you write?" Sal said. Reading and writing were a luxury Sal never cared about.

"I trade with the sailors, learn my letters," Rosa said. A shrewd businesswoman, but she was as proud of her alphabet as a school child.

"I need these words, *San Diego*, on the back of this old parchment," Sal said. He gave her an extra *peso* and rumpled the letter from Jimenez's Papá until it looked like the worn military pass he saw a soldier presenting on the dock.

Rosa took her time to print the words. "*Bueno*, heh?" Rosa said. She beamed, proud of her talents.

"*Muy bueno*, here, use the candle wax, press your ring into the wax until it looks official," Sal said. He could only hope these false documents would work. They passed the afternoon like two children, playing with letters and candle wax. Sal considered the idea of taking Rosa with him to *San Diego*. But how would he ever explain her presence to Blas, Father Serra or Brother David?

The next day Sal walked to the edge of town to retrieve the ox-cart hidden in the hills. A stench in the air reminded Sal that poor Jimenez rotted in his shallow grave nearby. He spotted two boys as he approached. "You there. Will you take three *pesos* for a day's work hauling this cart?" Sal said. He considered it a generous offer for two kids.

"Move your cart? What about your stinking friend in the ground, *Coronel*?" The boys said. Sal didn't expect the vagrant youth to answer so boldly. They actually tried to threaten him. His anger rose, and he raised a boot to kick them aside. Better yet, he could afford to use his *pesos* to bribe them to get the cart on the next vessel bound north for *San Diego*. They struck a deal.

At dawn, Sal waited near the space where the Spanish freighter docked. Impatient to get going, the boys with his cart waited close by. He spotted skinny Rosa standing near the loading ramp clinging to the arm of last night's customer, a young seaman. He saw her whisper in his ear and point in Sal's direction. Has she reported me? The little traitor, just let her try to stop me from boarding.

CHAPTER 19

Sea of Cortez, Baja California 1802

OLD MACIAS

Sal approached the dock, ready to offer his last *pesos* as a bribe to get on the northbound ship. Rosa clung to the sailor stationed at the bottom of the ramp. Could she be trusted with Sal's secrets? Waving Jimenez's military identification and the forged *San Diego* orders in one hand, Sal saluted with the other.

"Special envoy to the Bishop of *Alta California*, the Reverend Father Serra," Sal said. "Check your logs. Father Serra recently left this port for *San Diego*." Did he speak with enough authority to convince this sailor? Sal gave him a slight bow.

"There you see, I told you," Rosa said. Thrilled

to see Sal salute so officially, she responded with a little curtsey.

"Father Serra is expecting my services and this small cart of church goods in *San Diego* as soon as possible. I cannot lose any time, *¡vàmanos!*" Sal said. He imitated the bold tone Father Serra used when he made his demands at the *Presidio*.

"As I told you, he is an officer—*muy importante*," Rosa said. The sailor, anxious to please Rosa, returned the salute and clicked his heels as Sal stepped onto the ramp. Sal considered Rosa's help a minor miracle; she was an angel, after all. He reached for the *pesos* in his pocket. The boys followed him with the church supplies bundled on the cart. Sal boarded the vessel just minutes before it cast off.

His arrival, and his cart, caught the attention of three passengers on the crowded deck. Old men, muscular sailors, and boys toting bags, buckets, and blankets, crowded into the spaces between piles of cargo. "See the soldier?" a man named Jacques said.

"Damned colonial military," his companion, Jean Paul, said. He aimed a spit of tobacco juice overboard.

"One of those proud Spanish," a third traveler, Dumas, said. He shook his fist in Sal's direction. "They are losing their control here," Dumas said. He bowed with a flourish when he spoke of Spain. The mocking gesture caught Sal's attention.

"He's protecting something in the bundle of loot he hauled across the gangplank," Jacques said. "Did you hear him declare it was goods for a high churchman?"

"Yeah, right before he bribed his way on board." The three companions—Jacques, Jean Paul and Dumas—shared a laugh. "Standard church procedure," Jean Paul said. The men were squeezed between the packing crates and the ship's rail. The ship—really a barge—piled high with crates and barrels, rolled from side to side against the dock. Thick coils of rope and tangled seaweed draped the rails. Nets full of cargo, dried fish and packaged goods swung from the crossbars on the mast. None of the passengers had any privacy above or below deck. They squirmed on top of tarps and gunny sacks or between boxes and hoped the rolling sea would not shift them toward the crushing cargo.

"Let's get some liquor in him, get him to spill a little information," Dumas said. Sal tried to ignore them, but in these cramped quarters, he could hear every word. Their accent sounded strange, not Castilian Spanish or one of the Mexican dialects. Sal maintained his focus on the arid horizon. He only wanted to think about his rendezvous with his countrymen in *San Diego*. An old salt with a scope looked out in the same direction and seemed to read his thoughts.

"The passage north takes five days. Call me Macias," said the old man, Macias, extending his boney arm, "See the shallows on the other side of the straight? They'll send you to hell in a heartbeat." Not speaking to anyone in particular, he used a scope but seemed far too old to be a part of the crew. "For safe passage, we keep our distance. Keep your distance from those three French fools, too. God give us safe passage."

One of the three men observing Sal approached from behind and spoke with a gruff voice. "To the wind at our back," Jean Paul said. He offered a toast familiar to any seaman.

"Amen," Sal said. He inched around until he

faced Jean Paul, who was a few inches shorter than himself.

"Join us, soldier," Jean Paul said. He waved a bottle, offering a drink. As much as Sal wanted it, he politely refused. Who were these men who stood before him offering liquor?

"Bound for *San Diego*, or beyond?" Sal said. The three of them looked ragged and dirty, as ragged as he'd looked before the gift of Jimenez's uniform.

"Ay, we are, and ports beyond. They call us buccaneers," Jean Paul said. He never expected Sal to refuse the drink. "Bound for any inlet needs dredging, soldier." He tried to lighten the conversation with some humor. "We're the mules hired to clear the harbor. We are half men, half mule." His French companions laughed at his joke and continued to guzzle from their bottle.

"It's a wise man who holds his own council and refuses a stranger's liquor, especially if it's offered by a Frenchman," Macias said. The wise old man holding the scope was alert to the drinker's intentions. Sal acted like a disciplined soldier; he made a slight bow and backed away from the men. He had to remind himself he held an important commission from Father Serra.

He turned to look back toward the horizon. A reunion with his lifelong friend, Blas, filled his thoughts.

After several more days and more attempts to approach Sal with liquor, cards and other pastimes, the three Frenchmen forgot trying to start a conversation. They slinked between the other passengers, lingering dangerously close to unguarded pockets and purses. Whenever Sal turned his back, the Frenchmen brushed against his bundled cargo and tried to figure out what types of treasures he delivered for the church. They watched for an opportunity to snatch goods from the cart, but old Macias kept an eye on the men when Sal moved away from his cart. Macias was slow but sly. He was easy to overlook as a guard, or an ally. During the entire voyage, Sal took little notice of this aged protector, Macias. He watched for more dramatic signs and blessings.

The passage from *Mazatlán* to *San Diego* lasted five days. The sea blustered and threatened the over-crowded vessel, and the passengers found little shelter on the crowded deck. With each sunrise, Sal took note of the passing hills that displayed more greenery the farther north they traveled. On the fifth sunrise, the winds calmed to a breeze, and the ship cut a good wake. Gleaming silver dolphins appeared alongside, escorting the vessel northward. Sal convinced himself that their presence was a good omen for things to come.

CHAPTER 20

San Diego, Alta California 1802

REUNITED

The evening of the fifth day, the barge approached the landing in *San Diego*. The old salt, Macias, babbled on, "All ashore who's going ashore. Check your pockets; the Devil lurks in every port." The three shabby buccaneers scrambled overboard, like rats, before the ship dropped anchor. Their pockets bulged with stolen loot, threatening to drag them under. "Buccaneers, they say. Ha—pirates, all three. Watch them scramble for the secret caves in *La Jolla*," Macias said. Checking his pockets for Jimenez's papers and military pouch, Sal thought about how to explain his changed identity to Blas, Father Serra and Brother David. Macias muttered more warnings, "And another thing, watch them natives. Most are kind, but some big ones, *Tipai*, they call them, can get mean in a moment."

Sal paid little attention. He was busy scanning the dock where he spied a friar in a grey hooded cassock. The man was too stout for Father Serra, too short for Brother David. The cleric was standing among the few persons waiting on the dock.

"Need help with your bundle?" a crew member said. Sal wrestled the dilapidated ox cart away from its moorings on the deck. "Hold on until the gangplank is empty," the crewman said. Passengers crowded toward the exit, clutching their belongings. The departure continued with no order, no dismissal or checklist like Father Serra might require—just a mad scramble to leave the barge.

"It's a two-man job alright," Sal said. "God bless you sailor." The cart barely fit on the narrow exit. He wrangled it on the plank and across the swampy landing. Sal offered Jimenez's last *pesos*. "A tip for a good man, God's speed." It was first tip he ever gave anyone, except Rosa.

The robed cleric approached Sal. "Welcome *Coronel!* We prayed for supplies, you are our angel of mercy," he said.

"I'm no angel. You can thank Father Serra for these supplies," Sal said. He tried to see the face beneath the cleric's hood. "He commissioned me."

"Yes, yes, we are all commissioned by God, Brother," the cleric said. "I'm afraid Father Serra has already moved on to consecrate new Mission grounds in the north." The cleric stepped away from the shoreline and turned his back to Sal. His words were muffled by the hood covering his head. "I will receive the goods. Come, follow me," he said. This short round man did not lack authority. Sal noticed he spoke like the other Brothers, with a lot of flowery talk and offered no real help with the cart. Sal followed him, still struggling with the load of supplies. The chubby cleric slowed to catch his breath. His face was turned away but Sal could see him steady himself with his hands on his knees. The man's shoulders shook and he gasped for breath.

"To be honest, *Coronel*, you must be the most bedraggled soldier in all of Imperial Spain. What happened to you?" the Brother said. He gasped for air between every word.

Sal strained to hear his words. "What's that you say, Brother?" Moments ago, this same man called Sal a saint. Now he insulted him, calling him bedraggled. It dawned on Sal: he recognized the voice. The chubby Brother was Blas! The friends were reunited at last!

"And you are the fattest walking vow of poverty I've ever laid eyes on," Sal said. Blas still wore a ridiculous robe, pretending to be one of the Brothers. "*Un abrazo.*" He wanted to hug Blas, but too much emotion in public embarrassed him. Pretending to be men, but quarreling like boys, they grabbed each other in a welcoming bear hug.

"*¡Gracias a Dios,* you are here, my friend!" It didn't matter who said it first; they both thanked God. Sal knew he would remember this reunion as one of the happiest moments in his miserable life.

CHAPTER 21

San Diego, Alta California 1802

JOSEPH'S RAIDERS

"I never guessed you were the butterball on the dock," Sal said. Chubby from his cheeks to his knuckles, Blas's fat fingers bulged like mitts.

"Some mercy, *por favor*. You were not forced to walk to *San Diego* with that taskmaster, Father Serra," Blas said. His fat belly bounced when he spoke. "The man drove me like a mule. We stopped to baptize everyone who crossed our path. Thank God he moved on; we were half dead with his pious diet. After Serra left, I could eat everything the natives brought. The local tribesmen, the *Tipai*, convert every day. They bring us small game, wheat breads, fish, *todo delicioso*. We'll eat well tonight."

"Did you say Father Serra is gone?" Sal said.

He surveyed the desolate setting: scrub brush, sand, boulders along the cliffs. How would Serra even know what direction to head in? "*Pues*, invite me onto your estate, *por favor*. I can only imagine what you and Brother David have created here. Just like the old days at the Mission in México, heh? You, me and Brother David." Not too concerned about Father Serra, Sal had missed Brother David, a truly kind holy man.

"Brother David? *Pero no*, he's not here in *San Diego*," Blas said. He shook his head as he broke the news.

"Where is he? Do you have any word of him?" Sal said. His spirit sank to a new low.

"Of all the missionaries, Brother David is the most kind. No one would deny such a good man shelter. God will protect him, Sal, keep the faith," Blas said.

"Yeah sure, keep the faith. Just remember, you are a false cleric talking to a man impersonating a dead soldier," Sal said. He lost all hope of finding David.

"*¡Por Dios!* Dead soldier? For the love of God, Sal, don't tell me…," Blas said. He shook his head, unable to complete his sentence. How much had his time alone changed Sal?

"What are you trying to say? You think I murdered Jimenez?" Sal said. "Did you kill for that robe?" What kind of a friend would think such a thing?

"But the uniform, it is Jimenez's. ¿Sí?" Blas said. He lunged for the military satchel, opened it, found Jimenez's identification. "I knew you brought him along for a reason." He backed away from Sal in horror. "You planned this all along." He looked Sal over for a weapon, blood or any sign of his violence.

"Sure, it's Jimenez's uniform," Sal said. How could he remove the fear he saw in Blas's face? "You can't blame me. Jimenez died of fever before we reached Mazatlán. I tried to save him. I even buried him. I have a right to use his identity, just like you use a cleric's robe," Sal said.

"I want to believe you," Blas said. Having accused Sal of murder, he burned with shame. "Forgive me, amigo. This New World has cast its spell on all of us. One thing I know, God has made a way for both you and me. And now we are back together, for life."

"A spell? Don't worry about it. Maybe you and God can help me move this load," Sal said. He liked to tease when Blas got overly serious and religious. "I'm sure ready for some good food." The friends worked together to move the old cart toward the Mission grounds. They did not speak again until a stranger appeared on the pathway.

"Who is the man blocking off the trail?" Sal said. The most threatening native he ever saw approached. His hunched shoulders and beak-like nose reminded Sal of a vulture.

"It's Joseph, here to help," Blas said. He could be relied on to think the best of everyone.

"An Indian named Joseph?" Sal said. Something about the native man threatened Sal.

"Joseph is his baptized name," Blas said. "He helps us with everything and brings more natives to the Mission to work every day." Joseph stood astride the path like a man who owned the territory. His eyes were locked on Sal. "*Hola*, my friend," Blas said. He turned the cart and its contents over to Joseph's control before Sal could put up a protest. Other native men approached and formed a tight group around Joseph. Were they ready to assist or just eager to get a look at the new supplies? Sal wished he could understand what Joseph said to them in their native language. Each man studied Sal and his military jacket.

"They don't seem to be too happy to see me," Sal said. "That one big man would be enough to deal with, but his friends are all just as serious looking."

"Why are you always ready for a fight? Just leave the cart to them, Sal. Believe me, all the natives here want to help," Blas said. More tribespeople came into view as Blas spoke. "They're good fishermen and workers. The women weave. It's ideal territory for the Mission." Friendly or not, they were surrounded, so Sal followed Blas past the natives and beyond a line of bramble bushes marking the border of the Mission grounds. They headed toward a lone bell hanging from a rough scaffold in the middle of a flat dry compound.

"Where's the chapel, the workshops? This is nothing like the *México* Mission," Sal said. Blas appeared to be proud of the empty encampment. Beside the bell, a low-slung hut made of brush sat on the dirt. A pile of stones stood nearby. Scattered charcoal pits marked the location of recent campfires. What delayed the progress here?

"*Bienvenido*, welcome to our main dining room," Blas said. It looked more like a picnic ground. An open cookfire crackled with steaming clamshells, dozens of small red fish roasted on sticks and a basket filled with berries lay on a rough blanket sitting on the dirt. Several more Brothers made their way from the brush hut with baskets of bread and cheese. "It is my great pleasure to introduce you to the most revered Brother Luis Jayme." Blas's formal introduction sounded ridiculous in these rustic surroundings.

"*Gracias Señor*. You see, our new Mission requires much work, *Coronel* Salvador," Brother Jayme said. "The gift of tools and building materials came right when we needed it." Because of Jimenez's uniform, the Brother assumed Sal to be a soldier and called him *Coronel*. The men celebrated Sal and his oxcart with toasts and praise. Sal noticed all the Brothers were as chubby as Blas. "Now we can replace the thatched chapel walls with more sturdy stuff."

"We'll train Joseph and the others to use the tools and raise a roof for our dormitories," Blas said. Sal began to relax and eat with the clerics, but noticed none of the natives were welcomed to enjoy the meal.

"To the first Mission in *Alta California*—one Father Serra and the King will take pride in," Brother Jayme said. After the toast, one of the Brothers stepped forward to ring the lone bell for midday prayers. They all reached for their prayer books deep in the sleeves of their robes and began the chants Sal despised. While their heads were bowed, Sal took the time to look around and see if Joseph and his followers were near. He could not shake the feeling someone watched him closely.

After prayers, everyone prepared to return to afternoon chores. Right on cue, the native men reappeared, each man clutching a tool from the cart Sal delivered. Joseph kept a firm grip on the shovel Sal used to bury Jimenez. Another of Joseph's men stood with a sharp-edged hoe slung over his shoulder. A third man cradled an ax.

"Just look how eager they are to get to work," Brother Jayme said. He marched off like a captain leading his men into battle. Sal could not help but wonder, did the natives truly intend to assist? They followed close behind Brother Jayme with cautious glances left and right.

"Doesn't it seem odd to you?" Sal said. "Does Joseph ever let Brother Jayme out of his sight?" He watched Brother Jayme and Joseph walk beyond the bramble bushes.

"You worry too much. Just look, *mira*, this is how we will build the Mission," Blas said. Anxious to share the Mission plans with Sal, he reached for a charred stick from the cook fire and began to draw in the dirt. "Look—this shaded area is where we say mass now. These supplies will help us construct the first real chapel here."

"I didn't bring many supplies. Where does the timber come from?" Sal said. "I see no trees here." He wondered where Brother Jayme disappeared to.

"God will provide," Blas said in an annoying sing-song voice. "You brought the spades, and now the natives can dig the clay for adobe brick," Blas said. "Each day, they haul stones from the cliffs for a foundation. Father Serra left us all of these plans for the glory of God." Blas spoke with real excitement about the plans. Sal envied his commitment to something new and grew angry. Would Blas hear how doubtful and bitter he felt?

"You said all our other plans went wrong because of me. Maybe this plan will go wrong if I stay," Sal said. Blas followed someone else's dreams now, not like before. "Once you followed my plans. Maybe now you think you need to save me, like one of your Indian slaves. I did my best, but God didn't provide for me." Years of friendship were on the verge of being crushed into dust. Blas dropped the writing stick and took a step back. He made a quick sign of the cross on his forehead.

"Salvador Tenorio: remember our first risks?" Blas said. "We were boys, barely escaping our mothers' control, and it's true, we were full of *el diablo*. We called it curiosity." Blas paused, looking Sal straight in the face. "We schemed to steal food from the ship because we were hungry and desperate. You kept me from death in the prison and again on the long passage across the Atlantic. Remember how we sang for our supper when we reached the *Nuevo Mundo*?" They remembered and grinned. "Do you really think I blame you for anything or want to make you my slave?" Sal stayed quiet, ashamed of his attack on Blas. "No *amigo*. We were just boys. We owe our escapes to the grace of God. From tonight onward, we are men, and we will always be *hermanos.*"

"Brothers," Sal said. *"Lo siento,* sorry. How could I have doubted your friendship?" The two friends reached out, like men, to shake hands, but it soon became a boyish arm-wrestling match.

CHAPTER 22

San Diego, Alta California 1802

BLACK SMOKE

"We could make this place great together," Sal said. During the next three days, Sal and Blas imagined new plans for the Mission project as they walked around the proposed building site. A few of the native children giggled as they followed the *estranjeros*, foreigners, pointing at their light-colored skin, beards and Blas's green eyes. "If only our Papás could see us today. They were once amigos, like us."

"I've thought of Papá. I'm such a bad son. Do you think he is still alive?" Blas said.

"He's with the saints by now, *como mi Mamà*," Sal said. "Let's send a letter to the family, those still in *Yuste*. We can tell them, 'Sal and Blas are alive *en este Nuevo Mundo*.'"

"The Brothers write fancy script, let's ask them now," Blas said. He wanted to ease his guilty conscience and get right to work on the letter. They paused near a shaded area where the Brothers studied their scriptures.

"No, it can wait until the morning. Let's get some rest now. *Una noche màs*, one more night will not make a difference," Sal said. He was ready to sleep and dream about how many exciting possibilities waited for them in this new place. Sal spread out sleeping mats in the thatched hut, and they dozed off.

Choking with a dry cough, Sal awoke in the pre-dawn hours, trying to catch his breath. He heard noise and commotion outside the thatched hut. He thought Blas slept nearby. Thick smoke collected inside the shelter. "*¿Dónde esta, Blas, where are you?*" Sal scrambled outside to draw a clean breath. The compound was engulfed in turmoil. Brothers and natives battled flaming tumbleweeds and smoldering palm branches. The old cart that Sal brought from *México* and all the tools burned. The scaffold supporting the Mission bell sagged, about to collapse. Sal spotted Brother Jayme running toward the bell. "Where are you going? *¡Cuídate, careful!*"

Heading toward a group of natives, waving his arms above his head, Brother Jayme didn't hear him. The Brother attempted to warn the others to stand back from the heavy bell before it fell and crushed them. Moments later, he fell to the ground. Some of the natives rushed around him. But, to Sal's horror, they didn't help him escape the fire. They beat his body with burning clubs.

"What are you doing? Get away from him!" Sal said. He struggled to his feet, too far away to be of any help.

"It's Brother Jayme, stop, stop!" another Brother said. This man was fearless as he ran forward, trying to defend Brother Jayme. It was Blas! He struggled to reach Brother Jayme, and in seconds, he too laid sprawled on the ground. Native men beat Blas and also attacked other tribal converts. They moved like tall, dark shadows through the ash and continued to stoke fires in all parts of the compound. Still choking on the smoke, Sal tried to reach Blas. What could he do? Blinded by the ash, he could identify only one man who held his ground and looked past the wreckage. It was Joseph who stood and surveyed the chaos his men brought to the Mission compound.

"Let me at him," Sal said. Joseph guarded the bodies of Blas and Brother Jayme. Sal tried to move toward Blas to rescue him. Joseph and his raiders surrounded the space, swinging burning clubs and keeping everyone back. Sal crawled on his hands and knees. "I know about you: these men are not converts, they're under your control," Sal said. He was convinced Joseph recruited the men to win back the Mission lands. Sal gripped the dirt and felt heavy blows landing on his back. Pain shot from his spine through his legs. He had to make it to Blas and drag him to safety. All he could move were his arms and shoulders, which he used to drag his limp body forward. With just inches to go, Sal prayed to awaken from this nightmare. Then everything went dark.

Hours later, Sal opened his eyes to see the black night sky. His body lay outside the bramble bushes surrounding the compound. All was quiet except for one whispering voice, "*Vàmanos*, we go," a native convert slumped away. "*Segura ahora*, safe now." Had this man dragged Sal to safety? Where was Blas?

Sal crept back around the bushes to see a

charred, empty compound. Void of life, as black as the sky above. He stumbled along the Mission perimeter until he saw the slope leading to the harbor. His legs ached, but his heart was in more pain—this was the same pathway he and Blas walked on a few days ago. Sal told himself he'd find Blas at dawn and get him to safety near the water's edge.

At the end of the pathway, Sal began to feel his way along the boulders of the coastline. He slipped into a protected space between two gigantic rocks and fainted away in shock and fatigue.

After hours of fitful sleep, familiar voices awakened him. Not Spanish or English, but French speakers jolted his memory. He recognized these voices—the buccaneers from the *Mazatlán* voyage.

Jacques' men investigated the burned Mission grounds before dawn, foraging anything they could steal. The grounds were scorched—nothing and no one left. The men returned to the beach to report to Jacques. Sal heard the voices from his hiding place among the rocks.

"It wasn't any cook fire—they got cleaned out," Jean Paul said. "Let's move on; nothing here for us. But wait, what's this? A sorry-looking fellow tossed from the ocean." Three men stood over Sal.

"Let's throw him back into the sea. Maybe he'll swim home, ha, ha," Dumas said. The men grabbed Sal by the ankles and pulled.

"¡Ay no, no!" Sal said. His voice came out hoarse and weak. He had no strength, no boots, no uniform—only the Long Johns he slept in the night before.

"Give the poor man something to drink, Jacques. Looks like he's been through a rough time of it," Dumas said. The trio eyed Sal as he guzzled their liquor.

"We're not your enemy, man. You survived the fire. Drink up. Come along with us if you want safe passage out of here," Jacques said. Sal looked toward the Mission grounds. Could he still help Blas? He grabbed at the rocks trying to crawl toward the burned area.

"There's nothing there; I checked it myself." Jean Paul stood in Sal's way. "But look, do you see the light out on the sea?" They all turned from the Mission bluff to look toward the surf.

"Be quick. Strike a flint and let them know we're here," Jacques said. He rushed toward the shoreline. Sal struggled to his feet. "Quick, man!" Jacques barked orders. Another voice called out from the direction of the surf.

"Jean Paul? Jacques? Declare yourselves if you know the words..." the voice said. The three buccaneers responded in a chorus.

"Live by the sea!" they said. Jacques grabbed the burning palm branch, waving it in the direction of the surf. Sal thought he saw the vague outline of a boat.

"Die by the sea!" Offshore voices called back. Were these passwords? Two men sloshed through the water to the shore dragging a dinghy on a tow line. Sal didn't care who they were or even where they were headed. He just wanted to get away from the horrors of the previous night.

CHAPTER 23

San Pedro, Alta California 1802

PANTALOONS

"Who is this little girl in pantaloons?" a buccaneer said. The new arrivals laughed at their first glimpse of Sal in nothing but Long Johns.

"Give him a bottle of your whiskey. I guarantee he'll pay us back," Jacques said. Sal drank from a dirty liquor bottle while the buccaneers worked to retrieve their stash from a nearby cave. The liquor helped to wash away some of his grief over Blas. The stolen loot was dragged out of the caves and packed in crates, chests and burlap bags. Then the men hauled it to their vessel anchored offshore. Even a few live chickens squawked in one box.

"All aboard!" Jean Paul said. The men hauled

Sal onto the boat. He slumped over on the cramped deck, thick with scum and moss. The ship's sails were tattered and streaked with seagull droppings. He shut his eyes and pretended to sleep.

"I tell you he's the lad we saw in *Mazatlán*, the military man who held the cargo," Jacques said. He stood astride the deck as if he captained a fleet instead of this renegade pirate ship.

"You're talking about the soldier who refused our liquor for seven days? Now, look at him. He hasn't let go of the bottle," Jean Paul said. "Why keep him? He's no use to us. We'll move faster without him."

"Let him speak," Jacques said. He dumped a bucket of slimy water on Sal's head.

"Wha... what's this?" Sal said. He spat grit and seaweed out and tried to regain his focus on the company. Surrounded by their snarling faces, he became aware of the danger he faced. The Devil spoke in Sal's mind, "Listen closely, speak slowly. I know these sorts."

"I'm telling the boys you're an officer ... you guarded precious cargo for Spanish Missions, am I right, man?" Jacques said. He grabbed ahold of Sal's arm, testing his strength then checked

Sal's hands for the tell-tale blisters every working man carries.

"Missions? Where am I? Who are you?" Sal said. He stalled, slowing his words.

"I'm your friend, Jacques. We met in *Mazatlán*. You carried church supplies," Jacques said. His grin, far from friendly.

"Tell us your name or my mates will toss you overboard," Jean Paul said. His knife at the ready, Sal could see Jean Paul would take his life unless he proved useful.

"I'm Salvador. I don't want anything to do with the Mission or the Brothers."

"You see, he speaks. I'm telling you this man knows things, useful things," Jacques said.

"He's no good to us drunk, get him some grub and keep him awake, then maybe the Spanish dog can help us," Jean Paul said. He turned away from Sal and began to order the other men about.

"We're going to give you a disguise, Spaniard. You help us grab some of the galleon cargo, and there'll be a percentage in it for you," Jacques said. His words sounded full of swagger and false promises.

"Me? What about the real soldiers at each

dock and friars waiting onshore? They keep track of everything. They've got Mission Indians, mean ones; ready carry the load," Sal said.

"You see—he knows the routine, he'll fit right in." Jacques said. Clearly, he commanded the crew. By the looks of their cargo, he helped himself to unguarded goods in every port, then sold them for a profit in the next port and kept the best of the loot for himself. "Show him our sack of Spanish rags."

Dumas pulled tangled clothes from a burlap bag and tossed two Spanish regiment jackets toward Sal. A grey cassock, like the one Blas wore, lay wrinkled among the jackets.

"Where did this come from? A Brother's robe? I'm not part of your thieving," Sal said.

"You'll do as we say, or your little pantaloons will fill our costume bag. Now get dressed," Jean Paul said. He picked one of the jackets and pushed it in Sal's face. Sal weighed his options, counted the dangerous crew, and realized his chances of escape were few. If only Blas were here, they always found a way out of trouble. A vision of Blas's crumpled body at Joseph's feet filled his mind. He tugged on the uniform.

"You thinking of your friend, the little fat Brother?" Jean Paul said.

"You know about him?" Sal said. "Did you see him? This couldn't be his robe, could it?"

"Nah, we saw you two at the dock in *San Diego*. Did he go down in the smoke the night we found you?" Jean Paul said. His head sagged in mock grief.

"It's not our fault. Someone got to them before we could," Dumas said.

"What a fool. 'God will protect us' he used to tell me," Sal said. Blas's face and the Mission grounds, full of ash, blackened his memory.

"A holy man, heh? Takes all kinds," Jean Paul said. "One thing for sure, life's a curse and short for all of us." He gave Sal a slap on the back and raised his bottle in a toast.

CHAPTER 24

San Pedro, Alta California 1802

PIRATES

The buccaneers sailed, against the wind, for one day and into the night. "Say your prayers Sal; tonight, you meet St. Peter," Jacques said. He used a scope to spy on the busy port of *San Pedro*. Jacques, Dumas and Jean Paul huddled on the foredeck scheming against the small ports and the trading vessels they spotted along the coast.

"Just look at all the cargo lying on the dock," Jacques said. "Even better than the last time we were here." He handed his scope to Sal. "I've decided you and Dumas can do this job. Jean Paul and me will stand watch from the deck."

"Why do they call this place *San Pedro*?" Sal said.

"How should I know? It's your people who named it," Jacques said. "Listen, if a watchman gives you trouble, distract him from our business." Jacques laid out the plans. "First, load the new tools and hardware. Then, snatch shiny cargo—anything silver or brass—candlesticks, goblets and such." Jacques' orders reminded Sal of his days in *Ciudad de México* when he and Blas learned to make candlesticks while Brother David crafted silver goblets. Now, these buccaneers wanted him to steal something he had made with his own hands a few short years ago.

"Pay attention, Spaniard: you send the loot back to us on the tow line, or else. Then wait for our signal," Jean Paul said.

Their pirate ship anchored out of sight of the port. The plan included using the smaller dinghy to sneak out to the dock, then distracting the watchmen and making off with the merchandise. "When we wave the torch, you'll know we've got the goods. Then you get yourselves out, *pronto*. You hear me?" Jacques said.

"Aye Captain," Sal said.

"What about the natives, Captain? He's no good for the job, Jacques. How do we know what he says to the Spaniards? Let me and Jean Paul do it," Dumas said.

"It's just the *Tongva* band natives around here,

nothing to fear. I'll keep a watch on him; he's got no loyalty to Spain now," Jean Paul said. "Don't you get distracted, Sal. Jacques will slit your throat if you don't follow his plan." Jean Paul slipped a small folded cloth into Sal's pocket.

The fog rolled in, covering the moon. Sal and Dumas tried to get ahead of one another as they scrambled into the dinghy. It rose and fell with the sea swells. Dumas, an experienced oarsman, guided them. When they approached the *San Pedro* dock, Sal could see there were only two watchmen—one on each side with the new supplies between them. Jacques had guessed right; both guards struggled to stay awake. Sal and Dumas crept onto the dock at midpoint to survey the goods. One of the watchmen moved. What could Sal do to distract him?

"*Fumar*, smoke?" Sal said. He strode right up to the man in his military jacket disguise. When the guard looked at him, Sal moved to block the man's view of Dumas. He reached for the tobacco Jean Paul planted in his pocket.

"*Seguro*, sure, why not?" the watchman said. He was smooth-faced and younger than Sal expected. Taking advantage of the kid, Sal's hands shook while he attempted to roll a cigarette. The second watchman began to snore. Dumas lowered the goods onto the dinghy. Nervous, Sal tried to engage the young watchman. Without thinking, he began to hum one of Blas's favorite tunes.

"*Bueno*, a good old song…" the young man recognized it. At least it kept him distracted from Dumas' activities behind him.

Jacques and Jean Paul were nervous. They signaled too early with a bright flame from the main ship. The other watchman, an older man, opened his eyes. Dumas reacted quickly, hitting him with the flat side of a shovel and knocking him unconscious. Then Dumas dragged the shovel toward the younger watchman near Sal. The fellow hummed, unaware of anything but enjoying his cigarette and a song…whack! The young man sprawled out on the dock, looking a lot like Blas the night he fell onto the Mission grounds.

"He didn't deserve that," Sal said. "He's just a kid."

"He'll be ok," Dumas said. "They'll come to and make up an excuse for the lost goods." Dumas' eyes burned with an anger Sal had seen somewhere before. "If we kill 'em both, there'd

be a bounty on our heads. Come on, let's go."
Dumas wanted nothing more than to boss Sal
around and prove himself to Jacques and Jean
Paul. How could Sal be a part of this violence?

They escaped back to the pirate's schooner.
Anyone seeing Sal's actions would see the truth.
Salvador Tenorio had become a real soldier of
fortune: a pirate. He thought this life, what he
always wanted, would be more exciting. The
truth was, remembering Blas's song had been
the best part of the night.

CHAPTER 25

Channel Islands, Alta California 1803

TREASURE CHESTS

Long after stealing the *San Pedro* supplies, the pirates' luck began to change. There were fewer ships to rob. Tempers grew short. The men quarrelled among themselves, but Sal admired Jacques' daring ways—especially his control of the crew. Could it be that life among the pirates suited Sal's true destiny?

One grey morning, with little to eat and no fresh water, everyone on board grumbled about the low supplies and their next move. "Let's go ashore and swap. We've still got some of the *San Pedro* loot," Sal said. Maybe this time, Jacques would listen to him.

"Look at this Spaniard, a natural-born buccaneer," Jacques said. "You know, in tough times like these, the Portuguese sailors eat their own." His face half grin, half snarl. "Are we ready to draw lots for Sal's skinny little carcass, men?" Why did Jacques treat him like a kid?

"Jacques' humor turns ugly when supplies get low," Sal said. He should have known better than to say that to Dumas, who taunted him each chance he got.

"You know nothing about a man like Captain Jacques. You're only a kid: get to work, keep your mouth shut," Dumas said. Sal grabbed some rags to return to his swabbing.

"Listen here, Sal." Jacques bent on his knee and spoke to Sal in a low voice. "Listen here, Boy. If I was born one hundred years ago, I could have been a musketeer in my own land. Truth is, fighting for the good is always the best choice. But in these times, when our leaders turn against us, what can we do?" At first, he sounded sincere, and then he rose to his feet with his fist in the air. "Ha, you become a buccaneer! Right men? And I can tell you; there's not much loot this far north." He held up a faded map of the coast. His finger, the one with a ruby ring, traced the ship's route.

"Have you been north? Tell us about it," Sal

said. He imagined Jacques' risky enterprises.

"Nah, no regular ports nearby. *Monterey* is a good four days of rough sailing. I know what I'm talkin' about," Jacques said. "I read the sea better than a preacher reads his good book."

"I say we lay in wait, attack the next transport sailing south," Jean Paul said. His feet astride, clenched fists at his waist, he spoke as if he wanted to be in command.

"Why risk our lives for a few scraps? We'd need three vessels this size to stall an English frigate or threaten a Russian tub," Captain Jacques said. Sal looked from man to man seeing the competition between them.

"Hey, look at those small canoes," Sal said. He hoped to ease the tension. "Bet those Indians come from nearby villages with food, hides to trade, women too. I know. In *México* I traded church goods with the native people." Maybe he'd gone too far blurting out the secrets of his life. The others now knew where he'd come from.

"Trade for women, you say? Ha, don't you know, son, they are the most dangerous trade of all," Jacques said. He looked at the other men, trying to get a laugh out of them.

"Listen to the kid, Jacques: we've missed all the good raids since the full moon," Dumas said. "I'd swap one of these shovels for animal skins— we'd get real money." The men were desperate. Sal regretted pointing out the canoes, adding to the unrest. Captain Jacques needed to keep control of this vessel. They ended up drifting all day, hoping for something to come their way.

At dusk, the scenery began to change. The Channel Islands came into view, the first land like a tall ledge of rock overlooking the ocean. The island outlines played on Sal's imagination. What a good spot to hide a signalman with a flag. Sal imagined himself as a look-out sending warnings about sea raiders. This time he kept the idea to himself; he didn't want to risk sounding foolish.

"Remember the old days when we stashed good China silks on these islands? We gave the Russians a bloody battle on their last passage," Jacques said.

"I remember, but these men don't—they were just children back then," Jean Paul said. He stood shoulder to shoulder with Captain Jacques, showing the others his experience and importance. "Yeah, the islands—friendly natives, too. No Spanish devils to get in your way." Did he refer to Sal?

Sal dropped off to sleep, thinking about his last friend. He used the wadded-up monk's robe as his pillow. He dreamed of a sea serpent on the horizon, many times longer than their forty-foot schooner. Coiled on the ocean, the serpent's ridged back stretched north—the rest, swallowed in fog. "*¡Ay Dios—el Diablo!*" He awoke, yelling like a kid, "God chases me to the end of the earth, his serpent will swallow us."

Jean Paul shook Sal by his shoulders. "I'll tell your Mamà this pillow gives you nightmares. That's not a sea serpent, that's the ridge of our island, you idiot," he said.

"You mean, our bank vault in the sea," Jacques said. He rubbed his hands together.

"We've got treasure hidden there, son. Look below the ridge crest where seagulls flock."

"Treasure?" Sal said. He stood at attention, ready to collect his part.

"At ease, man," Jacques said. "All us buccaneers know the story of these islands. Even the Russians used their people, the *Aluetes*, to raid the *el agua de los Nicoleño*. Bad business for the locals.

"Keep a lookout: these days, it's those English raiders always around scheming for our goods," Dumas said. He guided the schooner toward a flock of gulls hovering over a cove. Hundreds of birds squawked overhead near the rocky cliffs.

"We'll smash on the rocks," Sal said. The ship moved too close to the gigantic rock wall.

"Who let this old woman aboard?" Jacques said. His eyes were wild. A flutter of pelicans soared above the cliffs. Dark shadows clung to the rocks. The entire vessel headed straight into a sea cave. Jean Paul struck a flint to light a torch. The sleek schooner moved further into the gigantic cave as it rocked on the sea swells. The cave swarmed with bats. Birds squawked above their heads.

"Will we fit? We'll get stuck," Sal said. Swallowed into the darkness of the serpent's belly, Sal's nightmare had come true.

"I got in, but there's not much time left," Dumas said. "This tide will change soon; we'll get trapped in here for sure." He struggled to maneuver the ship, a tight fit inside the gigantic cave.

"Come on; there's time. Go once around near the walls. Let me see where we left our crates,"

Jacques said. He hung over the railing, straining to see past the torchlight.

"What ya say?" Sal heard nothing above the noise of the birds, the bats, the incoming tide. "What's this?" He leaned over the side, reached for a wooden plank floating in the water, flat, narrow, the length of his arm.

"Give it to me," Jacques said. He grabbed the plank. "Damn those English dogs, get me closer."

"This crate must have broken open against the tide, the English never could have found our spot here," Jean Paul said.

"I'm robbed! Treasure from three voyages, stolen!" Jacques said. He scrambled over the side of the boat and waded in the shallows toward a sandy mound. His old treasure vault lay in ruins. "I'll skin 'em alive—make a sail of their hides," Jacques said. He stumbled over shattered treasure chests.

"Leave it be. Get back aboard, Jacques. The tide is coming in fast," Jean Paul said. The mouth of the cave began to fill with sea water. The whole crew called out to Jacques who raged on like a madman clutching at piles of sand.

"We can't wait any longer, give him this," Dumas said. He threw Jean-Paul a line.

"Here. Follow us out, or you'll die here. We'll catch those thieving English. Come aboard, man," Jean Paul said. Would Jacques come to his senses? Sal saw him on his knees, panting and pawing like a dog for any bit of treasure left behind.

"We can't leave him. He'll drown. He's our Captain," Sal said. He tried to jump overboard toward Jacques. Jean Paul grabbed him by the back of his pants, yanked him back on the deck, held him tight.

"He's lost his mind. He can't go on without the treasure. The sea will swallow him whole. When a buccaneer loses his treasure, he loses his life," Jean Paul said. He kept a tight grip on Sal. They watched in silence. Jacques never even saw them go. Sal's last sight of Jacque disappeared inside the cave.

When the tide receded, Jean Paul led the ship back into the cave to collect Jacques' remains. They pried his battered corpse off the cave wall and stripped off the seaweed. Back on the open ocean, the men gave Jacques a pirate burial, dropping his body overboard. Sal watched him sink and remembered so many others released to the sea. He thought about Jacques, Brother

Jayme, Blas, even Jimenez—all dead now. No one had any glory in the end. Holy men and scoundrels, the grim reaper dragged all into darkness. Jacques' corpse disappeared beneath the gray waters, just more fish food.

CHAPTER 26

Channel Islands, Alta California 1803

MUDDY WATERS

"I thought pirate stories ended with treasure chests full of gold coins," Sal said. He talked to himself as he scrubbed the deck on his hands and knees. With Jean Paul as captain, Sal expected empty pockets. "Where's this mad man taking us now?" He missed Captain Jacques as their leader.

Jean Paul tried to act the part. "Let me think on this." He stroked his beard, looking thoughtful. "I'll wager those Spaniards left cargo with the Indians." He stood tall, pretending to have hatched a brilliant idea. "We're going to find the loot with the natives!" He took credit for Sal's ideas about trading onshore. "We're going to find plenty of loot, men. Sal will get us past the Spanish soldiers, right Sal?" All eyes turned to Sal. He took his time before he turned toward Jean Paul.

"Aye, aye Captain," Sal said. He wanted to spit on the deck every time he called Jean Paul, Captain. Sal could have managed the schooner himself, if only Jean Paul gave him a chance. The voyage from the Channel Islands to the mainland proved easy sailing. A flat sea with no barriers, only the silver dolphins to escort them along the way. The rocky coastline barred their landing with no sign of a harbor or an open stretch of beach. Sal spotted native men sitting on the cliffs, their long fishing lines dangled in the surf. The fishermen seemed to ignore the pirate ship. Sal wondered, were they friendly or lookouts for the tribe? No one else thought they were important enough to mention, but Sal knew better.

"Look ahead to the muddy waters," Jean Paul said. "Muddy water means there's an inlet, a good passage." He looked at his crew, expecting obedience. "Oarsman! Release the dinghy. You take Sal aboard and head out. Follow the passage," Jean Paul didn't even know his oarsman's name. Why would anyone choose to take orders from him?

Sal crawled over the rail into the small landing barge, ready to get away from Jean Paul. Dumas rowed them toward the muddy water. Jean Paul got one thing right, the inland passage appeared right away, wide enough for a Spanish landing party. The quiet strokes of the paddles maneuvered the dinghy against the current. Well upstream, Dumas brought the craft to a halt.

"I'll climb the bank and go on foot from here. You hold our dinghy steady in this spot," Dumas said.

"You're leaving me here, all alone?" Sal said.

"Scared, Spaniard? I've got to see what lies beyond," Dumas said. Steep banks rose high on both sides of the river. The small dinghy felt cramped. Sal's thoughts were dark; he imagined the boat like a coffin. The longer Sal waited, the more he thought about the muddy river below him. What a deep burial ground it would be. Did he hear the grim reaper call his name from beneath the water?

"Sal, Sal," Dumas called out as he swam back toward the dinghy. "The Spanish dropped their supplies here, alright." He flung a leg over the side of the barge then struggled aboard. "Beyond the bank, there's more Indians. Their women are sorting through cargo crates. There is a monk, too. He's following me. Hurry!" Dripping wet, he panted out his news.

Sal heard a booming voice calling from the river bank. "Did you bring us the tools you promised? The anvil..." a man onshore said. Sal struggled with the oars. He tried hard to get the dinghy underway. Dumas tugged the oars away from Sal and took control of the dinghy to begin their escape. Sal could not believe it: he recognized the voice. Brother David?

"Let's get moving, Sal," Dumas said. "He's spotted these uniforms and thinks we're soldiers from the galleon." Sal's rubbery arms pulled in the anchor line.

"The tools! We need them," the man on the shore shouted.

"*Nos vemos, pronto*, see you soon," Sal said. He lied, promising to return. Maybe responding in Spanish would slow the monk, maybe even get rid of him.

"What did you say to him? We're lucky there are no real soldiers here, only a pesky monk,"

Dumas said, his voice full of worry and suspicion. "We've got to snatch this cargo quick."

"Bad idea," Sal said. "The last thing we should do is return for the cargo."

"You try to explain that to Jean Paul when we return empty-handed," Dumas said.

"I'm not coming back here. Those Indian women will tell the men, probably the same fishermen we saw on the cliffs," Sal said. He felt unnerved by the narrow river, the high muddy banks—worst of all, the familiar voice of Brother David, who he once considered a friend. He could never know Sal had become a pirate.

Jean Paul kept a torch lit aboard the schooner to guide Dumas and Sal back to the ship. Sal was trapped between the Captain's lust for the goods and being found out by Brother David.

"Give a report, man. Did you get some loot for us?" Jean Paul said. He called out as the dinghy neared the ship. The crew behind him looked anxiously at Dumas and Sal.

"Like you said, Captain, perfect. Half of the goods are still in crates," Dumas said. He cautiously started his report with the good news. Sal kept quiet. He regretted not going alone to scout the passage.

"We can go back, snatch the cargo and move on free and clear," Dumas said. He looked down at Sal, still sitting in the launch, and dared him to disagree.

"It's an easy passage, a one-man job," Sal said. He already hatched a new plan. If he went back alone, there would be no one to keep an eye on him.

"You volunteering to go back alone?" Jean Paul said. "It will leave more room in the dinghy for loot."

"Hold on a minute, Captain: someone spotted us," Dumas said. He didn't want to be cut out of the assignment. "A crazy old monk hollered about tools or something. He thought we were part of the Spanish convoy, ha, ha, ha." The Captain and crew laughed at the old monk thinking of them as Spanish soldiers. Jean Paul smelled treasure ahead and wasted no time with his decision.

"I'm putting Sal in charge now. Let the old monk think we've got his tools. Sal, surprise him and give him a bullet in his back after you've stolen the goods. Right?" Jean Paul said.

—*—

CHAPTER 27

Alta California 1803

SAVE HIM!

"Take this gun," Jean Paul said. "It's all on your shoulders now, Sal." He pushed Jacques' old revolver into Sal's hand. Sal's fingers shook as he tried to take hold of it. He could use it now and get rid of Jean Paul. He wished he could make the captain his target, not Brother David.

"I'm not going to fool the monk if he gets a good look at me," Sal said. He hid his face from Jean Paul, pretending to fumble with the last button on the faded Spanish uniform. Sal hoped no one could read his murderous thoughts.

"Dumas could go back with you," Jean Paul said. He stooped to get a look at Sal's face.

"I said I'd finish this job alone," Sal said. He planned how he'd abandon the pirates, confident he could row far enough for Jean Paul to lose sight of him, but not far enough to be spotted by Brother David. Then he could make a run for it.

Sal said, "Farewell mates," and he meant it. The fog rolled in so thick it covered him like a shroud. The gun lay beside him in the dinghy. He couldn't see or hear anything but the faint ripples of the inlet against the dinghy.

The river reeds made a low swishing sound. "Sal, Sal, Sal." He resisted the feeling that someone called his name. His imagination ran wild. Did Blas's ghost hide in the fog? Sal spoke to the ghost, "Why'd you run out and get yourself killed?" Sal said everything he wished he could say to Blas. "You left me behind, all alone. We were supposed to stick together." To his surprise, Blas's ghost answered.

"*Oh yeah? Why'd you let those thugs hurt the watchman in San Pedro?*" Blas's spirit wouldn't let Sal think straight. "*There was never anything like that in our plans. I saw you steal those supplies.*" The voice seemed so real; Blas must be hiding nearby. "*You found new friends, too, like the girl in Mazatlán? Come on, Sal, I thought you were a better man!*"

"Rosa? How'd you know about her? You can't judge me. You pretended to be a friar, and it got you killed. I've got a real monk to deal with now, good old Brother David," Sal said.

"*To deal with? Remember, he's the only one who helped us in México,*" Blas' spirit said. His voice began to fade away. He said one last thing, "*Don't shoot Brother David; he needs you to save him.*"

"Save him! Save him!" Sal heard the voice of a boy nearby.

Then, a second boy spoke, "Help me!" The fog cleared, and Sal spotted two kids, struggling with a bullfrog caught in their net. They argued like he and Blas used to. When they noticed Sal, a stranger holding a gun, they dropped their frog and ran away, calling for help. The boys called attention to him; what choices did he have left? Should he row out to the pirate ship and face Jean Paul without any loot? Should he confront Brother David with this gun? Fate made the decision for him. The boys returned with six native men and Brother David.

"So, you did return," Brother David said. He stood at the top of the riverbank and gazed down toward Sal. "Did you bring the tools this time? You could have waited until daylight." Sal kept his head turned away. The monk didn't give any sign he recognized him. Many years had passed since they worked side by side at the Mission in México. The native men approached the dinghy, their angry faces turned on Sal.

"You are here to help, *¿deveras?*, right?" Brother David said. He spoke in a calm tone.

"*Si, gracias, hermano*, yes, thanks, brother," Sal said. He hid Jacques' gun behind his back. The dinghy shifted in the water, but Sal stood so the natives could see him as a strong man. Let them try to overtake him. He positioned himself ready to use the revolver if needed.

"Sit, soldier, as a sign to my friends if you mean us no harm," Brother David said. He didn't recognize Sal or know why he approached them at night. He spotted the gun. "Throw the *pistola* behind your back in the river—we don't want it in the wrong hands." Sal slipped the gun under his coat.

Blas used to say that Brother David acted 'wise as a serpent but gentle as a dove.' He knew how to negotiate between these uneasy natives and aggressive Spanish soldiers. But he didn't recognize the man he spoke to as Salvador Tenorio.

"Chilly tonight. Come to the campfire with us, get warm. There's food, *bienvenido*, you are welcome here," Brother David said. He walked away from the riverbank. Sal kept his face hidden as he stepped out of the boat. Just one gun against these natives and a monk didn't offer much protection. Clutching Jacques' revolver kept Sal focused on what he planned to do.

The gathering around the campfire reminded Sal of the nights he spent in *San Diego* with Blas. The women served steaming food in small bowls carved from gourds. Here, everyone ate together. The two boys from the river played nearby. The native men relaxed, surrounded by their families. Sal kept imagining Blas's ghost lurking in the shadows, worried about Sal's next move. He thought about the spirit's words at the river, "*Don't shoot Brother David, save him.*"

Brother David kept staring at Sal. He tried to place him. "*Sabes que*, you know, I'm waiting for those tools so we can begin work on this Mission site," Brother David said. Why didn't Sal think to bring the shovels and tools he stole from the *San Pedro* dock? Before Sal could answer, Brother David took two giant steps and confronted Sal, face to face. "Tell me this, soldier: when did the blacksmith, Salvador Tenorio, become a *Coronel* in the King's infantry?" He finally recognized Sal. Now he teased him. "By some miracle is your *amigo* Blas Bonilla also a lieutenant, ha, ha, ha?"

When Sal heard him say Blas's name, he reached for the gun. A bullet at this distance would be fatal. He couldn't stand to hear David joke about Blas. Sal's anger exploded, but Brother David reached for him with his strong blacksmith arms. He got hold of Sal and captured him in a bear hug. "*Cálmate* Salvador, calm down, I'm joking. God has saved you and brought us back together! I want to hear the whole story," Brother David said.

CHAPTER 28

Alta California 1803

TWISTED CROSS

"Blas died." Sal said it out loud for the first time. The words rang in his ears, his heart thumped with pain.

"But, h-how did this happen? W-when?" Brother David said. Hands pressed together, even his prayers could not bring Blas back.

"He died trying to save Brother Jayme," Sal said. "You heard about the Indian attack at the *San Diego* Mission?" A grim image of the native man they called Joseph, standing over Blas's body flashed through his mind.

"You were there? Blas must have been so brave," Brother David said. Choked with guilt, Sal hesitated before he responded. He glanced toward the pirate ship hidden offshore, then looked back at Brother David.

"I wanted to help, but I couldn't do anything for my friend," Sal said. The confession caught in his throat. Brother David put a hand on Sal's head. Trembles, humiliation and relief battled in Sal's body. David and Sal cried together.

"Let's walk away from here, Sal. Blas waits nearby," Brother David said. He bent to take a small bundle from the campsite. Why did he say that? Did Brother David hear Blas's ghost, too? Sal peered into the shadows surrounding the camp. He noticed the natives kept their distance; gathered around the fire, they looked away from him. "Come with me. We'll take the hill behind the camp."

Talking about Blas's death relieved Sal's grief. Feeling more relaxed, he left the pistol under a blanket then followed Brother David toward the hill. They began a slow climb on a sandy slope. Dry scrub brush swept at their ankles along the narrow trail. Unburdened by his confession, Sal talked nonstop.

"We thought you abandoned us in *Ciudad de México*. We were slaves in the *Presidio* stables. I figured, well Blas too, figured out a way to escape. What a horrible trek with Father Serra on his return trip to *Alta California*," Sal said. His memory mingled with his imagination. He wove a seamless plot. "Remember our old rickety ox cart? I dragged the same *carretera* with *Coronel* Jimenez." He deserved some credit for his hard work. "We searched for our own water, food, kindling, even the route to the coast." Sal skipped the stories about selling church goods along the way and stories about *pulque* and women. "Jimenez knew a lot, but he did not survive in the end." He stopped himself before saying anything about his days with the pirates.

"I can tell that you carried a heavy load, Salvador. *Que làstima*, how sad," Brother David said. "Traveling with a broken heart is one of life's greatest burdens." How did Brother David know this? "This man, Jimenez—the one who died—was he your age, named Daniel?" He put his bundle on a large flat rock at the top of the hill. "We never really travel alone, Sal."

Sal ignored Brother David's question about Jimenez, "*Si, si*, I mostly traveled alone." Did he already know about the pirates? "From this hill, can you see all the ships passing this way?"

"*Deveras*, true, from here I see everything, *como Dios*, like God," Brother David said. "*Mira*, look around. That is why this hilltop is the place where we will build our new Mission. I already use this flat rock as my altar." Brother David set a crooked pair of candlesticks on the large rock table and pointed to some scratches on their base. "Do you remember these?"

"Our makers' marks from the foundry in *México!*" Sal said. Holding a memory in his hands, Sal studied their stems—a twisted cross roughly molded in the silver. "Look at the scratches. Here is Blas's mark and mine too." The foundry seemed like another lifetime. Sal's life felt twisted like that cross. Why did Brother David keep these?

"I could not bring myself to leave behind your first crooked attempts at candlesticks. No church would ever use them, but they were precious to me," Brother David said. He took another look at the horizon.

"What did you mean about Blas being here?" Sal said. He stepped between Brother David and his view of the ocean, hoping for the fog to roll in and hide the ship.

"*Cada noche,* each night, I light these candles and ask God to protect you and Blas, my brothers from *México,*" Brother David said. He lit the candles on his rock altar. "It's how we come together in prayer, every night, *como tres amigos,* three friends." He gazed at the flames.

"But your prayers didn't protect Blas," Sal said. A few candles and an old man's prayers were not going to bring Blas back.

"You're right. His bravery, trying to help Brother Jayme, is something to give thanks for," Brother David said. Sal bit his tongue. Maybe bravery, maybe stupidity. Blas didn't give Sal a chance to help him. He knew Sal would never risk his life for Brother Jayme.

"Y *tù,* and you Sal? I consider your courage to go on, after such a terrible experience, an answer to my prayers as well. You came all this way to find me." He grasped for some sign of hope.

"I'm not as brave as you think," Sal said, ashamed to reveal his own stealing, drinking and lying. What kind of make-believe world did this *loco,* crazy monk live in? Even near the lit candles, the darkness enclosed them. Sal looked again toward Jean Paul's pirate ship on the horizon. He heard something moving on the pathway. A native man approached them.

"That man stole my *pistola!*" Sal said. He

reached for the nearest weapon, a rock.

"*Hermano* David: *tomol.*" The big man carrying Jacques' gun shouted at Brother David. Did he figure out Sal's plan to rob them? Sal rushed toward him, ready to launch the rock.

"Hold on Sal, *tomol* is their word for canoe," Brother David said. He followed the native's gestures toward the sea. "Look, we've got visitors. Do you happen to know who it is?"

"There's something I need to tell you," Sal said. He kept an eye on the man with the gun. The time for the truth had come, no time left for pretending.

"*Dígame*, tell me Sal," Brother David said. He spoke to the native in his own language. The man took a step back, keeping the gun out of Sal's reach.

"Those men are here to do you harm," Sal said. He did not tell Brother David everything, especially the part about being a pirate.

"¿Y *esta pistola*, is it their gun? D-did they send you here to harm us?" Brother David said. His stutter made him sound foolish. His glare threatened Sal more than the gun.

"The truth is, I'm a pirate, not the boy you remember from *México*. Not the man you pray for," Sal said. He hung his head like a little boy, *un niño*.

"A-and you've come to steal from the ch-church? I can't believe this," Brother David said. His voice, the slow, low growl of a wounded animal.

"You don't understand. Those pirates rescued me when Blas was murdered. They took me in. Y *la iglesia*, what's the Church ever done for me?" Sal said. He avoided Brother David's eyes. What a stupid excuse. Why'd he ever come back here?

"If you want to s-steal this rock or this hill, you're welcome to it," Brother David said. "There's nothing else to s-steal, *nada*. Don't you understand?" Brother David grabbed the gun from the native. "You're already dead, Sal. I can see those pirates stole your s-soul." He pulled the trigger. Two bullets flew into the air. "They've used you against your own b-brothers." It scared Sal to see the holy man act like this. "Satisfied? Your friends will believe you've completed your mission. Maybe they'll even think you m-murdered me." The empty gun hung at his side.

"You should have used one of those bullets on me," Sal said. "I'm the same liar you met in *México*." Why try to argue with the monk, a crazy man? After the gun went off, David's stuttering stopped.

"True, you're the same. You are nothing but a frightened boy struggling to survive. I know exactly what that's like," Brother David said. He slammed the gun on his rock altar. The burning candles fluttered.

"How could you know? You're supposed to be a holy man: educated, privileged. You chose to be here, to do this work," Sal said. He sounded tough but tears streamed from his eyes. "I came here as a prisoner: a peon, forced onto the damned ship," Sal said.

"Life is not always what it seems. You heard my awful stutter. It has plagued me all my life. I know what it is like to be ridiculed as a fool." Neither man looked at the ocean or the gun. They looked only at each other.

"My own grandfather, embarrassed and ashamed of me, turned me out and sent me to be a servant for the priests. He abandoned me," Brother David said. Sal couldn't believe what he heard. The same story Jimenez told about *Tio* DD, the stutterer. Why didn't he know this about Brother David? Did Blas know it? "You wonder why I took you and Blas in when I knew you were not really blacksmiths? Why I let you travel with me to *Puebla*? Why I told you my secrets about the library, the codex?" Sal remembered their first meeting. He and Blas thought they were smarter than Brother David. Stunned, he said nothing. "I met a monk who treated me with kindness when my family abandoned me. I wanted to do the same for both of you. I never thought you would betray me."

Candlesticks with a Twisted Cross

CHAPTER 29

Alta California 1803

DARK MAGIC

"Come with me and see how we deal with pirates," Brother David said. Sal stumbled through the dry chaparral, following Brother David past the cook fires. The monk would never be a match for Jean Paul and the crew. What did he think he could do? "These are not the first pirates we've seen. Low supplies and hunger plague all the sailors who pass this way. Give them food, and they move on." His voice offered no charity, only resignation, and scorn. The frog trappers, the two native boys, scampered toward the water's edge carrying baskets of fish and nuts to Sal's dinghy. The natives loaded it with their own food supplies.

"Brother David, you are in danger. They will come after you," Sal said. He waded into the water toward the boat. Two men, with black mud smeared on their faces, secured the barge.

"And you, Sal? Will you return to your pirate friends or stay here?" Brother David said. His voice trembled. Did he struggle to stay in control?

"I know these men. Captain Jean Paul will come to kill you at high tide," Sal said. He pulled on the boat, but the natives kept him from boarding. "What's on their faces, some kind of war paint?" Sal longed to make a quick escape.

"If you stay, they will guide the boat back to your friends. They wear mud to hide their faces," Brother David said.

"You've got to let me go. I'm no good," Sal said. The river water chilled Sal, body and soul. *Will you walk away from another friend? Brother David needs your help,* Sal heard Blas's ghost beg him to stay.

"God will forgive you, no matter what you do," Brother David said. "But we would welcome your help, Sal." He reached out a hand to give Sal a blessing. "Let the men take the boat to those pirates. We need you: please stay." The boat glided toward the open sea. The native men pushed it as they swam close to the waterline.

Sal panted, paddling like a dog behind them.

"Tule," one man said. He pushed a hollow reed toward Sal, showing him how to use it like a straw to breathe underwater. The barge cut a path through the reeds, on a direct course toward Jean Paul's ship. Beds of kelp surrounded the boat, hiding the natives and Sal. He knew Blas's spirit wanted him to stay. Another part of Sal knew this might be his last chance to escape. Near the ship, he heard the pirates talking.

"They shot our Sal and sent us this food as a peace offering, the dirty cowards." Sal recognized Jean Paul's voice. The other pirates reached toward the lone dinghy full of food.

"How'd they move the boat, Captain?" the crewmen said.

"Those heathens use dark magic. There's probably a hundred of them on the hill watching us. We'd never stand a chance," Jean Paul said. Hidden behind the kelp bed, Sal listened to the crew. He realized they never planned to wait for his return.

"I say we leave this God-forsaken place to the savages," the oarsman said.

"You can never trust a Spaniard or an Indian," Jean Paul said.

"I'd say this is enough food to get us back to *Mazatlán*. Turn to it, man," Jean Paul said. Once their bellies were filled, they set sail. Sal and the two native men swam back to shore. The same two boys who first saw him in his boat now waited for his return. Holding out Jacques' empty pistol, they wanted to know more from their new guest. Sal fumbled with the gun and started to teach the boys the Spanish word for gun, *pistola*. They reminded him of curious kids, like he and Blas in their boyhood. By the time he looked out to sea, Jean Paul's ship—and Sal's life as a pirate—had disappeared.

CHAPTER 30

Los Osos, Alta California 1804

BEAR HUNT

Sal struggled over his decision to remain with Brother David, even though he received a welcome into the small camp. Brother David gave him time to adjust to life with the group. For many months he gathered food supplies and learned how they crafted tools and weapons. He became more comfortable with the native converts and enjoyed the company of the children. Sal guessed Brother David didn't share all that he had to say. After many months in camp, the truth came out.

"I lied when you first came to camp, Sal. Now I must confess," Brother David said. "I told you Father Serra left to start a new Mission. The truth is, our Brothers in the north are starving: The King cut off our supplies. Even worse,

Father Serra has taken ill. I hate to admit it, but we are stranded here in *Alta California*. We need a miracle." Their little hunting party followed Paciano, a strong leader and trailblazer among the men. They collected food to replace what they gave the pirates in exchange for Sal's life. "Those Spanish cargo boxes you planned to steal were our last supplies." He rolled wooden rosary beads between his fingers.

"You're not worried, are you? I once saw how Father Serra got additional Mission supplies in *México*. He's fearless. If anyone can make it happen, he can," Sal said. No wonder Blas's ghost urged him to help Brother David. Damn, why didn't he return to the pirates when he had a chance?

"Sal, the King ordered troops out of *Alta California* by the end of the year—the missionaries too. Spain suffers with other wars, Lord save us," Brother David said. He wiped the sweat off his brow and made the sign of the cross on his forehead. Sal kept a wary eye on the muscular man leading all the others. Could they trust him? He remembered another strong native, Joseph, who murdered Blas and Brother Jayme in *San Diego*. Sal would not let that happen again.

The dark woman, the most beautiful female in the camp, walked close behind Paciano. She walked with those same two young boys, the froggers, at her side. He longed to know more about her.

Brother David walked slowly, dragging his feet. He followed Sal and saw what caught his attention. "I can see she intrigues you. She is Paciano's wife, Salina," Brother David said. "When she is baptized, I will call her Mary, because she is most faithful to her husband. She and her family are a few of the remaining Salinan band." He reached for Sal's arm to slow him down and pointed toward Paciano. "You ought to be paying attention to where we are headed. Paciano is an expert guide and hunter. He moves his clan to a new campsite every season."

In the late afternoon, the group made camp on the edge of a meadow where the setting sun cast round shadows on the earth. The men and women spoke to one another in low tones as they laid their mats and prepared their clay cook pots. "Why do the natives keep muttering those words, *los osos*?" Sal said.

"*Los osos*, they fear the bears," Brother David said. "Many dangers lurk here after dark. The bears come out each night. They claw big holes to gorge on the tule roots." Sal helped Salina's boys gather pine needles to cushion the sleeping mats. Determined to get her attention, he entertained her sons and pretended to be a lumbering bear. The three of them acted out a hunt. Everyone laughed except their father, Paciano.

Salina stayed busy passing lengths of rope to the men who strung bows, while others sharpened arrowheads. Sal tried to keep his eyes off her fine young body. He couldn't allow himself to get distracted by a good looking female, especially one who belonged to such a big man. Paciano spoke to his men in their native language. He handed Sal the first bow and arrow ready to use. The arrowhead felt sharp but too small for a big bear. For the first time Salina spoke to Sal, her breath sounded soft and urgent, "Los osos," she said. The men made a small circle around Sal and Brother David. Paciano stepped forward and grabbed Sal by his shirt.

"Does he want to fight?" Sal said. Were his desires for Paciano's wife so obvious? He turned to Brother David, ready to make an apology.

"Just take off your shirt, Sal," Brother David said. He seemed amused, and surprising Sal, pulled his own robe off his shoulders. "This is their preparation for hunting, the bay leaf ceremony." Women stepped toward them, holding bay leaves. They brushed the leaves over Sal and David's bodies. Salina herself, brushed Sal.

"Do we smell so bad?" Sal said. He felt embarrassed and thrilled by her hands so close to his skin.

"Without the leaves, we smell delicious to the bears. During the hunt, these bay leaves cover our scent. They protect us from a bear attack," Brother David said. After the rubdown, the women piled the stripped sage branches in a tangled barrier to hide the hunters from the bears.

"I can protect us from the bears—just give me a chance to use the rifle," Sal said. Emboldened by Salina's attentions, Sal wanted to be her defender. He had no more bullets for Jacques' old revolver, but one last Spanish rifle remained in the supply box.

"How do the natives know all this?" Sal said. He noticed how the men and women focused on separate tasks. Their knowledge of the surroundings impressed him.

"They learned from their parents, grandparents and great-grandparents who lived here for hundreds of years. It's their land, Sal. We learn their ways," Brother David said. The courage and determination of the natives reminded Sal of Captain Jacques. A man he respected, commanding others: the kind of man he wanted to be.

The bears entered the meadow at midnight: the largest came first, followed by the females and the cubs. "There's enough meat for all the Mission sites, enough for the soldiers too," Sal said. He counted twenty bears. Paciano squatted close by. He poked Sal's shoulder and put his hand over his mouth. His motions seemed to say: shut your mouth, just watch. The animals pawed the ground to unearth the plant roots. Once the bears ate their fill, they began to return to the woods. One old bear lingered behind the rest. A team of native men crept out with long twines tied in four lasso hoops. They laid the hoops between the bear, distracted with his eating, and the branch barrier. The other men became anxious and shifted around behind the branch barrier, straining to see the animals, ready to begin the hunt.

Brother David listened to the natives and translated their instructions to Sal. "You see the last bear, the straggler? Paciano says that bear is our target," Brother David said. "God provides, but we can give him a little help. Go ahead and get the rifle now, Sal."

"I'm ready," Sal said. He reached for the rifle and grabbed extra ammunition pouches. "I've got enough powder to shoot two or three of those big bears." He leaped out of the protective branches moving toward the remaining bear. Paciano and Brother David pulled him back.

"Sal, be careful! This bear is our only target tonight," Brother David said.

"I've got this rifle, and I know how to use it," Sal said. He ran his palm on the barrel of the big gun. "Those arrows will only graze him, but I'll make a clean kill with this, then go after more."

"Stop, Sal! Only kill the straggler, then the other bears will feel safe to return," Brother David said. Sal sensed Salina watching him, too. His excitement rose as he imagined the glory of his conquest, being the man who killed the bear and dragged it to camp. The beautiful Salina would cook it afterward—a feast and a hero's celebration.

Brother David broke into Sal's fantasy, "The men know what to do." The kill belonged to Paciano, the man whose leadership Sal wanted to challenge. The bear, as big as a boulder, moved toward them. It lifted its huge head, long teeth and claws dripping with saliva. The arrows flew and slowed the beast who moved so close. It slowed as the lassos snared the front paws. When it growled, Sal felt its hot breath on his face. The arrows hung limply from his fur.

"Shoot now!" Blas's voice echoed in Sal's ear. Sal struggled to raise the rifle. His arms were weak, and his body shook, making his aim impossible. No longer a distant target, the bear appeared like a massive wall directly in front of him. If it fell forward, it would easily smother him. His hands were too shaky to pull the trigger. He felt a strong man step behind him to lend support and help him grip the rifle. Together they pulled off a shot. Blown backward by the rifle blast, the two men fell in a tangled heap. The bear let out a roar, then lurched forward just inches from Sal. He heard a second shot from a distant rifle. The bear fell, a dark trail of blood oozing from its ear. Who shot that second rifle?

"*Los osos*," the man at Sal's back said. Paciano helped him to his feet. The other men approached the dead bear. The women stood back talking, excited. Brother David looked beyond the bear toward the ridge where the second rifle fired.

The bear hunt was over, but no one—not even Salina—paid any attention to Sal. He watched Brother David walking toward the marksman who made the final shot, a lone soldier with a rifle. The hunt did not end the way Sal had hoped. No one celebrated him as the hero. He called out to Brother David, "Did you see? Paciano helped me." Why would such a man let Sal take the lead?

"Yes, I saw," Brother David said. They both looked toward Paciano, who regaled his sons with his account of the face-off with the bear. "I saw a man focused on the needs of the tribe. Yes, he helped you, and God helped all of us."

Instead of victory cheers, the tribe gathered in silence around the dead bear. It reminded Sal of a funeral. One man used a reed flute to play a slow, sad tune. The others sang in honor of the slain animal. The women swept the space around the bear's fallen body and sprinkled a few leaves near his massive head. Sal remembered Blas's body lying still on the earth in *San Diego*. Blas deserved this type of gentle send-off to the next world.

———✻———

Bear Hunt

CHAPTER 31

Los Osos, Alta California 1804

THE MAP

Brother David stood on the hillside overlooking the camp, talking to the soldier with the rifle. Two men joined them, one in a bright military uniform. The hunting song concluded and the natives prepared to skin the bear. Salina stepped forward and assigned tasks. She pointed to the carcass, selected the right tools and mimicked the procedure, instructing the others. The tribe used every part of the bear, all handled with reverence. Salina and Paciano were truly the leaders in this tribe. Sal stood aside while others stripped the bear meat and prepared to hang it for drying.

Brother David rejoined the group followed by the men from the hill. "This first bear is for the tribe and our Mission family," Brother David said. He spoke to the armed soldiers, one decorated with metals and ribbons. "Captain Portola, may I introduce our heroes, Paciano and Salvador Tenorio." Was this Captain the miracle Brother David prayed for? Sal greeted the soldiers with some caution. They wore uniforms he could not identify.

"Without your final bullet we might have failed," Sal said.

"Not so, it was you two men who were face to face with certain death. You did not waiver," Capitan Portola said. "We can use brave men like you on our expedition to provide food for our troops."

Brother David interrupted, "We are called to share what God has provided, but our commitment is to the Missions first." Sal never knew him to withhold Mission resources from anyone.

"Pardon me Brother, without the soldiers the Missions would not be safe," Capitan Portola said. He stood erect but did not meet Brother David's eyes.

"Without God the soldiers are unprotected, sir," Brother David said. He held the crucifix hanging from his neck to emphasize his words.

"Let me explain, we represent the territorial transition, Governador Fages of *México*," Portola said.

Brother David cut him off, "The Governor?"

"...has commissioned us...," Capitan Portola said. He clenched his jaw.

"We are all subjects of the King of Spain here, aren't we?" Brother David said. He would not give way. The conversation volleyed back and forth between the two willful men. Sal waited, uncertain which man would win out. He decided to interrupt their competition.

"Did you make a plan?" Sal said. He knew Brother David always wrote his plans. Maybe this would show Capitan Portola what a wise man he faced.

"Why, yes, of course," Brother David said. He knelt to spread a parchment on the ground. "We are here, the next Mission site is here, thirty miles north," Brother David said. He pointed to a faint line on a map of all the *Alta California* Missions. His marks between the sites showed the travel time needed to move on foot from one site to another. Everyone—even Paciano—looked at the map, appearing to understand the writing and symbols.

Sal felt caught in the middle. He spoke to Capitan Portola. "Brother David asked Paciano and me to make these deliveries to the Missions. After that, we can meet your men here, and join your hunt." Sal looked from Brother David to Paciano then to Portola to get agreement. "You will not find a better guide than this man." Sal put his hand on Paciano's shoulder.

"Let me see this," Capitan Portola said. "Can I count on your word and the loyalty of this native man?" He reached for the map and gave Paciano a wary glance.

"Hunt," Paciano said. He knew one word. He jerked his shoulder away from Sal's hand and stomped his foot. That stomp sealed the deal. Next, Capitan Portola did a strange thing. He shook hands with Brother David and Sal, but instead of reaching out toward Paciano, he removed one of his battle ribbons and held it out as a gift. The rest of the tribe was looking on with great interest in the map and the soldiers. They cheered Paciano when he held Portola's gift high above his head.

Several evenings later the women collected the strips of bear meat, now dried into jerky, and packed it for distribution. Paciano and

Salina separated from the tribe for two days. Sal imagined them sharing an extended farewell. Sal only shared a goodbye with Brother David.

"Blessings on you Sal, your cleverness and bravery will provide the food the Missions need. Paciano knows the way. I'll stay behind this time," Brother David said. He moved slow with a limp in his step. He covered himself with an extra blanket slung over his shoulders.

"You know, I began the hunt with a plan to impress Salina," Sal said.

"You are ready for a wife, Sal, but not her," Brother David said.

"I know that now. I'll work with Paciano and Portola's expedition of Mexican transition soldiers. What a strange life this is," Sal said. He followed Brother David to a quiet spot.

"God is gracious, Salvador Tenorio. He sometimes surprises us even after we have given up our dreams and lost our best friends. You've earned the right to light our candles for prayers tonight," Brother David said. "Let me warn you, even good fortune can carry difficult experiences." He still carried those same crooked candlesticks.

✳

CHAPTER 32

Mission San Antonia de Padua 1804

PACIANO STANDS ALONE

The next morning Sal and Paciano set off to deliver bear meat to the Missions following Brother David's map. They headed in the direction of the third Mission founded, *San Antonio de Padua*, thirty miles north. Sharing their load of water and bear meat jerky, they walked the first miles in near silence. "The gun," Sal said. They pretended to disagree about who would carry the gun. He and Paciano could not communicate about anything aside from pointing out an occasional lizard or a trail of ants.

"*Mio*, David say me," Paciano said. He enjoyed teasing Sal about the gun with the few Spanish words he knew. Alone on the trail the two of them learned to get along. At first, they settled their differences with a tug-of-war.

After days on the road Paciano pushed Sal toward toppled logs and boulders, anything that could be used as a table. They positioned their elbows, clasped hands and began to arm wrestle. Paciano won the arm wrestling the first few days. As Sal became stronger, the leg wrestling began. They both enjoyed it and Sal welcomed the competition with his new friend. Sal began to talk freely as he walked. Paciano tried to teach Sal new words in his native language. Their respect for one another grew.

The terrain began to change. Lush tule plants disappeared. Dry plains and dusty hilltops appeared, everything covered with sun-crusted earth. According to the map they moved further from the coast in order to find Mission *Padua*.

They walked thirty miles in three days, carrying a heavy load, making camp every night. On the third day Paciano pointed out a low hilltop with a few trees. "Salina," he said.

"You're lucky. You have a good wife and two fine boys. I have no one," Sal said. He could make such a confession knowing Paciano could not understand his words. In truth, he never expected to envy an Indian, but this man became a true friend. Sal began to trust Paciano as he once trusted Blas. Could he be pointing to the place where he and his wife met and married? This was what Sal really wanted to know about. What were the native ways of courtship, marriage and mating? Could he ask?

"You, Salina...," Sal said. He smiled and thumped his palm over his heart. Paciano nodded. His slight smile let Sal know he understood his question.

The territory near *Padua* was so dry and so far from the sea, Sal thought it a mystery why Father Serra made this place his third Mission settlement. Then he saw hills in the direction where the sun rose. At their base stood a faint line of green tree tops. He remembered Jimenez's lesson: the trees mark a river—follow the river and you will find the people. A portion of low stone wall appeared to Sal before he saw any church. A robed Franciscan worked alongside native men to assemble rocks around a deep pit: a well.

"Brother Pieras? We bring greetings and supplies from Brother David," Sal called out. The words startled the workers who turned to see Sal and Paciano. All the men, including the Brother, had leathered skin stretched tight over their gaunt faces. Their long limbs and angled bodies reminded Sal of the lizards he had spotted on his journey. Paciano was the first to offer their water vessel to the workers.

"Praise God," Brother Pieras said. His voice croaked from his dry throat. After a long drink he offered the only seats available. "Sit here," he said. He motioned to the large stones gathered to rim the well.

It was Paciano who wasted no time, but opened a packet of the bear meat jerky to offer to the Brother and the native workers. Sal supposed the men would consume the food as quickly as they did the water, but they did not. The lizard image appeared to Sal again as he watched the Brother and the native men frozen in place, holding the jerky on their outstretched open palms. He and Paciano shared expressions of uncertainty. Who were these strange men in this isolated place? The minutes stretched on, sun glaring down, the earth completely still. Finally, the silence was broken.

"God is good!" Brother Pieras proclaimed and

the eating began. The men began to talk. They motioned to one another and tried to include Paciano in their conversation though he did not understand their language. When Paciano could not respond the other native men moved some distance from him. "Who is this servant you brought with you? He is not like the men here. Can he be trusted?" Brother Pieras said.

"Paciano is no servant. He is my friend and an excellent hunter." Sal was surprised by these suspicious words from the Brother. "If it were not for Paciano we would not have this bear meat to share."

"In any case, my men will watch him closely." Brother Pieras's head bobbed as he chewed the tough jerky meat. He glared up at Paciano from time to time. "You must have come from *Rancho* Duran in the north. *¿Que no?*"

"No, we come from the south, near the place of the bears, *Los Osos*. Brother David sent us to share these supplies," Sal said. He tried to hold his temper and speak politely to the rude Brother. He wanted to remind him that the food in his mouth was a gift and he should be thanking Paciano, and himself, rather than acting so suspicious. But Sal turned his thoughts to

Brother David. "He sends you greetings and his prayers for your…" Given the desperate look of these men, Sal was about to say 'survival'. But he stopped in time to say, "prayers for your success."

"*Ah si*, Brother David, *el herrero*, who stutters, ha ha. I remember him well from our time in M-*México* together," Brother Pieras said. Sal was shocked by his mocking tone. He was ready to grab the bear meat from their hands and walk away. "Stay the night. Your Indian man can sleep outside. We will keep a guard on him" By now the other natives had picked up stones and sticks as they eyed Paciano. Sal felt he could sleep for days, but not here among these unfriendly faces. Paciano stood alone, his broad shoulders thrust back. He must have understood the insults, but his expression did not change.

Sal drew in his breath for control and replied with false calm, "*Deveras*, in truth, we must move on. We are bound for this place Brother David called Mission *Soledad*," Sal said. "Do you know it?"

"Ha, you would be wiser to head direct to *Rancho* Duran where there are civilized people. You will find none of that in *Soledad*," Brother Pieras said. Without the decency of a simple traditional blessing, "*Adios*," Sal and Paciano picked up their supplies and began to walk.

It occurred to Sal that he had not truly heard a word of thanks from Brother Pieras who eagerly shared their water and jerky until he sensed that Paciano was somehow different from the natives he knew. It had been a long time since Sal's experiences in *San Diego*, where he first witnessed one band of natives attacking converts and the Mission Brothers alike. This life was hard enough, just surviving. "Why are men so ready to make new enemies?" Sal spoke to Paciano and had the feeling his words were clearly understood.

CHAPTER 33

Nuestra Señora de Soledad 1805

"CHUT-TUS-GELIS"

"*Soledad* means loneliness in Spanish." Sal repeated the name of the next Mission for Paciano, though he could not figure out how to convey its sad meaning.

Paciano repeated another word, one that was unrecognizable to Sal, "Chut-tus-gelis." Sharing their gifts of bear meat jerky was not as easy as Sal had expected. Brother Pieras's bad treatment of Paciano at Mission *Padua* still angered Sal. What could he expect here at Mission *Soledad*, the lonely Mission? The heat rose from the dry soil beneath his sandals. A nagging wind blew sand and ripped at the map that guided him and Paciano to their next destination.

The sound of a bell brought them to the

Mission. Miraculously timed between the gusts of wind, Mission *Soledad's* lone bell rang out. Paciano heard the clanging first and turned toward it. "Thank God," Sal said. "I couldn't take another day of this heat." One hundred steps off their pathway they saw the low silhouette of the chapel at Mission *Soledad*.

"Brothers, *bienvenido*." A robed skeleton of a man stood before them. "You are welcome. Come take shelter with us." Sal hesitated before he entered the chapel. This time he wanted to make sure the welcome was genuine and included both he and Paciano.

"Chut-tus-gelis," Paciano said. He held his palm open before him and nodded, first to the natives assembled in the chapel, then to the Brother. Raised hands, palms out, shot up in every direction. It was a welcomed sight and Sal breathed a sigh of relief as they entered.

"Come and rest with us friends. We have little to share but shade, God help us." The robed cleric led the way. "Brother Sarria, *a sus órdenes*, at your service." His hunger was visible in his sunken cheeks and parched lips. Sal flushed with the joy of having something of value to share with this man who was in real need.

"Your shade is a gift and we too have something to share. Salvador Tenorio, sent by Brother David. My friend and guide, Paciano, here." While he spoke, Paciano was quick to unpack the jerky and distribute it all around.

"Our Brother David in the south? Praise God," Brother Sarria said. "*El Señor* Paciano, I see you know our *Chuttusgelis* brothers. We are honored to have you among us." Now Sal realized the significance of Paciano's word. It was their tribal name. He smiled to hear Paciano given the title of *Señor*. As they sat together in the shade of the small chapel Sal heard more of Paciano's history from this feeble Franciscan.

"The trail you walk was here long before this Mission. The churches came after the first peoples, following their trail. My guess is that your friend, Paciano, hunted on that trail when he was a boy with his father. That is how he knows the names of our people." Sarria stopped his story to catch his breath. He was not an old man, but a shrunken soul. His elbows and knees jutted out of his robe. He blinked his eyes to keep his focus on the guests. Two children attended him with water and he was revived to speak again.

Paciano spoke and motioned toward the other native men. They passed his words to Brother Sarria. "You continue north to see Duran? He is a good man. I have been waiting for someone to take him this message." He reached into his sleeve and drew out a small folded packet. "Duran found this trail as a young man. He respects the history of the first peoples in this territory." He handed the packet to Sal and seemed anxious to continue his story.

"Duran once brought his baby girl to be blessed by the people of the trail. We named her Maria Theresa and the *Chuttusgelis* sent one of their own with him in friendship, the little girl Ria." Sarria leaned back as if he was preparing to sleep. "Promise me, whatever happens, you will give this to Duran." Sal inspected a scrap of parchment wrapped in the packet. It was blank except for a squiggled line. "This is the *Soledad* brand. Duran will be sure the Mission's native converts share the herd and the land when I am gone." Sal began to ask where Sarria was planning to go in his weakened state. Then he realized he was hearing the last wish of a dying man. Everyone in the chapel leaned in to hear Sarria's whispered words.

"Others have no respect for this history. Watch. See who comes with an open palm and who travels with a fist. The first follow the tradition of gift giving as you have done today, my friends. The others bring only death." Sal knew he had experienced both. Death at the *San Diego* Mission, and the fist of the pirates raiding the coastal settlements. Shame flushed over his cheeks. Did Sarria know his sins?

"You are now blessed to bring gifts, Salvador." Brother Sarria's breath rattled in his chest. "I have waited for you to continue the story of this land. My life is coming to the end."

CHAPTER 34

Monterey, Alta California 1805

A Toast

After three weeks on the road, Sal and Paciano prepared to make the last delivery of bear meat. Brother David's map marked a *rancho* near the Mission *San Carlos* located in the busy *pueblo* known as *Monterey*. El *Señor* Duran's *rancho* was known for its vast land holdings and fine breeding cattle. "We should have brought gifts for the two little girls at *Rancho* Duran," Sal said. Everyone seemed to know this man Duran. His watchmen gave Sal and Paciano a hearty welcome. Word had spread of the food supplies they carried. The Duran household had prepared guest quarters for the men and planned to host a celebration to honor their arrival. As Sal and Paciano settled in and rested after their journey, two women worked in the rancho kitchen.

The kitchen was a bright spot in the center of a sprawling adobe building. *La Señorita* Maria Theresa, now seventeen, was the only heir of *El Señor* Duran. She bent over a large butcher block table as she practiced making a display out of pink and yellow garden flowers. She struggled to prop up the blooms, surrounded by feathery ferns in a clay pot. This was a task her childhood companion, Ria, did so easily.

"My flowers will never be perfect like yours, Ria," Maria Theresa said.

"Let me finish this, you dress for the guests," Ria said. She was growing impatient. "You can play at decorating with flowers, but I have real work to do." The Duran family was so different from Ria's tribal clan, but there was real affection between Ria and Maria Theresa.

Maria Theresa played hostess at all the social events at the *Rancho*. The Duran's hosted regular *fiestas* at the time of harvest, *fandangos* after cattle branding and always, special dinners after holy masses. But Ria managed to avoid the guests and stay secluded in the kitchen. Ria used this excuse to stay hidden near the warmth of the mud brick oven. She enjoyed sorting the familiar spices and grains from her tribal territory. From the kitchen she could overhear their serious talk about the *pueblo* becoming the seat of power for this new Mexican government. No one seemed to remember the first peoples, her people, the *Chuttusgelis*. "Go make yourself beautiful, *hermana*," Ria said.

"*¿Para quien?* Beautiful for whom?" Maria Theresa said. Ria was used to listening to her childhood companion's high-minded rules for suitors and marriage. The young lady proclaimed strict requirements. "My future husband must have a true love for the people, not just his own authority," Maria Theresa said. She stood with her hands on her hips, chin held high.

"You have too many rules, Maria Theresa. Trust me, the right husband will soon be seated at your father's side," Ria said. Both young women were approaching the age to marry and start their own households. Ria was realistic about her dependence on *El Señor* Duran. Inside his house her secret duty was to keep a lookout for her tribe's interests. She learned to hide her bitterness about her people being driven from their ancestral home to make way for *Rancho* Duran with its fancy parties and important visitors.

The tribal leaders trusted *El Señor* Duran, and she must also. "In this house, your father makes all the rules. Prepare yourself to accept the man he chooses as your husband." At that very moment, *El Señor* Duran prepared to greet his guests. The *rancho sala* was arranged with fancy dishes, silver and candles. A place in the center of the table, set for twenty guests, was reserved for Maria Theresa's flower arrangement.

"*Pero, Señor* Duran, what do you know about this man, this Salvador Tenorio?" an officer in a fancy uniform said. He hovered outside the dining room delaying *al Señor* Duran from his other guests.

Sal prepared to enter the *sala* for dinner. When he heard his name, he paused on the patio where he could listen to the conversation. In this new *rancho* society Sal overheard questions about his character. He longed to prove himself respectable.

"This Tenorio fellow is nothing but a delivery boy, *nada*. They say he travels with some filthy Indian," the officer, Lt. Gomez said. He hunched over a short round man with a bald head, *El Señor* Duran. "Inviting this ruffian into your home, with your daughter present, is unwise. I'd never forgive myself if anything ever happened to her." Lt. Gomez continued his criticism of Sal.

"Calm yourself, Gomez. Tenorio has proven himself. Even Capitan Portola has invited him to join his expedition," *El Señor* Duran said. "You've seen how the church honors him with special masses. The Indian sometimes goes with him too, *tambien*."

"That only proves that Tenorio has fooled everyone. Remember, he is Spanish. Don't let him make a fool out of you," Lt. Gomez said. He flicked bits of lint off his uniform and tugged at the hem of his jacket. He wanted to display his powerful position as a Mexican military officer tonight. His goal was to make Maria Theresa Duran his wife and her father's property his own.

Duran was used to young men who claimed to love his daughter but were equally smitten with his land and cattle. "It's you who try to fool me, Gomez. *¿Verdad?* True? You tell me you love my daughter, but I believe you love my *Rancho*, my land, even more. Can it be you desire my cattle more than my Maria Theresa?" *El Señor* Duran said.

"You are wrong, father," Lt. Gomez said. He leaned in closer to *El Señor* Duran.

"I am not your father. I have enough people to take care of as it is." *El Señor* Duran stood, and put some distance between himself and Lt. Gomez. "You have no idea how hard it is to run a *rancho* this large: take care of the people, the livestock, the government agents who have their hands in everything."

El Señor Duran converted his scowl into a pleasant expression when he finally stepped into the dining room and greeted all his guests warmly. The meal was about to begin and *El Señor* Duran stood at the head of his table taking his place as host. He motioned to Sal to sit in a place of honor on his right.

"*Coronel*, you have arrived with enough bear meat to save us all. A toast, everyone, to our guest of honor, *Coronel* Salvador Tenorio," *El Señor* Duran said. He waved his glass around the table toward the assembled guests.

While *El Señor* Duran offered compliments, Sal glanced at the grand dining room. Twenty guests surrounded a fancy candlelit table full of delicacies. He couldn't believe his great fortune. He remembered his time as a prisoner, then the days when he and Blas impersonated blacksmiths. Now, here he was, introduced as an honored guest. He couldn't shake the feeling this high society held new dangers. Fancy plates, napkins, silver and fancy people. He observed a complicated mix of Mexican ranchers and soldiers, plus over-worked natives.

A long moment of silence passed when all the guests turned toward Sal before he realized he needed to make some comments. He stood on shaky legs. "*Gracias, Señor* Duran," Sal said. "The truth is, I share credit with many fine native hunters. Call me Brother Sal, *siempre a sus ordines*, at your service."

"As you wish. *Amigos*, we all thank God, for our guest and for this fine meal," *El Señor* Duran said. "My daughter, Maria Theresa prepared a delicious feast. We hope you'll enjoy another meal with us soon, Brother Sal."

Que milagro, what a miracle for Sal. He remembered those days he waited to enter a church behind the friars, honest and dishonest alike. Now he had the respect of the host and attentions of his *rancho* staff. A beautiful young woman served the meal. She leaned close to his shoulder to serve him. She smelled like vanilla.

"I've been eating nothing but bear meat. I know I'll enjoy this meal," Sal said. Lt. Gomez watched Sal closely from the distant end of the table. The officer made a lot noise getting to his feet, puffing out his chest strewn with metals and ribbons.

"Another toast, to the true citizens of our native land, *México*, and to the prosperous years ahead," Lt. Gomez said. Sal's Spanish blood boiled to hear the King's rule in *Alta California* dismissed. But the guests murmured their approval. Lt. Gomez made a special show of leaning forward with a formal bow toward Maria Theresa, the young heiress graciously serving her father's guests.

Sal realized the woman was *la hija del Señor* Duran, his daughter. She was not the little girl he was expecting. For a moment he was distracted, but he could not let Gomez's subtle insult against Spanish rule, and himself, go unanswered. He took a deep breath and stood.

"*Otra*, another toast, to the lovely daughter of our host, *La Señorita* Maria Theresa," Sal said. It was the first toast he ever made; a daring move, to publicly recognize the beauty of a single woman he had never met. It was the best way to upstage Lt. Gomez. After all, the boastful officer had referred to Paciano as a savage and then insulted Spain.

"*¡Bueno, bueno!*" The other dinner guests stood to cheer Sal's toast to Maria Theresa. She stood back from the table, blushing and gazed at Sal from across the room.

After the guests had reseated themselves, *El Señor* Duran leaned toward Sal and whispered, "Lt. Gomez intends to marry my Maria Theresa. Like her mother, God rest her soul, she has her own headstrong ways. Already, she has resisted proposals from wealthy men."

During the rest of the meal, Sal could not take his thoughts off Maria Theresa. He watched her as she circulated among the guests. Of all the lovely things in the *Rancho* Duran *sala*, she was the most precious. She possessed beauty, independence, and wealth. How quickly and hopelessly Sal desired her attention. The dinner chatter continued all around him. Sal's uniform and his new social status pushed him into an uncomfortable corner of Mission and *rancho* society. He could overlook the veiled insults and false compliments, if only Maria Theresa would consent to speak with him. How could he compete for her attentions? He had no estate, not even a father who stood by him. He made a quick calculation: his new reputation as a hunter and hero might help his case. Later that night, after dinner, Sal and Paciano returned to one of *Rancho* Duran's bunk houses for their night's lodging. Sal continued to think about the charms of Maria Theresa. With only one more night as guests at *Rancho* Duran, Sal decided to practice what he would say to her.

"I have no right to ask, but, ah, will you consider me as a suitor?" Sal said. He felt ridiculous talking out loud in front of Paciano who never understood him. But his friend listened with a sincere expression on his face as if he sympathized. Sal wanted to make his feelings known to the young woman, if only he could muster the courage. There was no time to waste. Sal was unsure of when he would be returning this way.

Amused by Sal's nervous attempts to express himself, Paciano grinned and actually strung four words together for the first time. "Ask woman, not Paciano." It was his longest sentence since the men began talking.

"Well if you're so smart, go with me to dinner tomorrow," Sal said. "You know *El Señor* Duran invited us both. Don't disappear again." In truth, Sal didn't want to go alone to the next dinner. He needed a friend. "They eat chickens, you'd like it," Sal said.

Paciano didn't think of the birds as real food. "Eat chicken—be chicken. Paciano eat bear," he said. Paciano managed to hide before every special mass or public meal held to celebrate the bear meat deliveries. Sal understood— Paciano enjoyed visits with the local natives while he ate with the wealthy ranchers. At least the two of them enjoyed each other's company. Soon they would be hunting bear together with Capitan Portola's troops. They trusted one another completely.

The final night of their visit at *Rancho* Duran, Sal hesitated before he approached Maria Theresa. There were too many people watching. Everyone asked about where his family came from, this Spanish bear hunter who befriended Indians and called himself Brother. At first, Sal enjoyed his new popularity, then he wished for some privacy and less public attention.

At the end of the meal Sal sought out Maria

Theresa, "Can we talk alone?" Sal calculated this would be his last opportunity.

"Who invites me?" Maria Theresa said. "The soldier, who is not really a soldier? The Brother, who is not truly a Brother? The hunter…?" Why did she seem so eager to challenge him? Beyond her words, her smile revealed her eagerness to speak to him. He paused to gaze on the beautiful, fascinating woman, then realized she waited for his answer.

"Who asks? The man who traveled the world to find you," Sal said. The words slipped out of his mouth before he could think about them. It sounded more romantic than he intended, but just as romantic as he truly felt. He watched her reaction. She seemed pleased and moved past him humming a tune that was vaguely familiar. She continued to move around the room gracefully, pausing to make polite comments to the guests and serving sherry to all the male guests at the dining table, strawberries to the women.

Then she circled back a second time toward Sal. "Follow me when I return," she whispered. Sal noticed her father, *El Señor* Duran, and Lt. Gomez watching them. The older man held a slight smile on his lips. Gomez scowled and sputtered insults gesturing in Sal's direction. Would *El Señor* Duran ever approve of him as a suitor for his daughter?

Maria Theresa stepped into the kitchen and returned, still humming, with a small silver tray with one serving each of sherry and strawberries. She leaned toward her father, "Brother Tenorio will take his sherry on the patio. I will keep him company," she said.

"The patio?" Lt. Gomez pushed his chair away from the table.

"Excellent, Maria. Lt. Gomez and I will finish our conversation in here," *El Señor* Duran said. Sal stood to follow Maria onto the patio.

"I hope you enjoyed your meal," Maria Theresa said. She laid the small tray on a ledge.

"More than I can say. What is that tune you hum?" Sal said. He breathed in the sweet smell of the garden jasmine and felt slightly dizzy. *Look at her, take her hand*, he told himself.

"Just a tune I learned from a poor old lame Brother. He ministers to the sick at the *Monterey* hospital. Brought from another Mission— *San Diego*, I think. And how did you enjoy the company tonight?" Maria Theresa said. Still, she maintained a cool challenging tone.

"Truthfully, I did not enjoy all the company,"

Sal said. "I don't think some of your guests enjoyed my company."

"On this *Rancho*, only my father's opinion matters." She turned to face Sal squarely. "He has heard so much about your bravery. I'm sure he wishes you were his son. I can tell," Maria Theresa said.

"And you?" Sal said. Hoping she would not call him brother, he pressed forward.

"I do not think of you as a son." Her lips parted in a breathtaking smile. "I agree, we should see you more often," Maria Theresa said.

"Next time I will make a very long visit," Sal said. His real interest was picturing himself returning to Maria Theresa with a proposal and a ring. Did he make his meaning clear? All the while the name, *San Diego*, echoed in his mind.

"When a man returns to his true family, we do not call it a visit," Maria Theresa said.

She resumed her humming. That tune, one that Sal was sure he had heard before. Then it struck him, it was one of Blas's songs!

CHAPTER 35

Monterey, Alta California 1805

A NEW BEGINNING

The delivery in *Monterey*, now complete, was the last stop on the map Brother David had charted for Sal and Paciano. Though Sal longed to stay and see if the lame man at the hospital was really Blas, he and Paciano were due to report to Capitan Portola for the official expedition. They had just enough time to return to see Brother David, Salina and Paciano's sons once more. On the seventh day of traveling they could see a new white cross peaking over the horizon. Brother David's church on the hill appeared complete. They looked forward to enjoying a brief reunion with the Mission family.

First, Sal delivered his official report about the bear meat distributions. He saved his serious personal business to discuss with Brother David afterward. "We've promised Paciano's boys they can go with us on our next delivery after the hunt," Sal said. Did Brother David remember long ago when Sal and Blas accompanied him on his blacksmith deliveries in *México*?

"Are you heading back to *Puebla* in search of a certain native woman?" Brother David made a joke, but Sal could never underestimate his spiritual gifts and insights. He, too, remembered those days, as well as Sal's fascination with *La Señorita Xichete*, the woman who offered her family codex to Brother David for his secret library. It seemed so long ago.

"Not to *Puebla*, but yes—there is a woman, and something else," Sal said. "How do you know these things? Her name is Maria Theresa Duran." He said her name with tender care and surprising affection.

"Thank the good Lord, Salvador. I know you deserve a bit of pleasure in this life," Brother David said. "By God, you've proven yourself a courageous and faithful brother." His eyes widened expressing his curiosity, "*Dígame todo*, tell me more. What other news do you have?"

Sal hesitated; uncertain of news so big it could

change his life forever. First, he shared the real possibility that it was Blas who ministered at the hospital in *Monterey*.

"I have heard these stories of the lame Brother who shares his songs of mercy," Brother David said. "I never dared to think it could be our Blas."

"Soon I will know for certain. I must return to Maria Theresa and her father," Sal said. He didn't know what he should say to a celibate Brother about his real feelings for this woman. "Maybe she will have me as a husband. But, what do I know about running a *rancho*? A woman and a *rancho*—it could be too big a job for me." His anxiety poured out.

"You are no longer a boy. Others will depend on you, it's true," Brother David said.

"If she and her father, *El Señor* Duran, consent, will you perform the marriage here in the new Mission?" Sal said. He wanted Brother David's approval.

"With many blessings, if my service continues," Brother David said. His eyes reflected the worry in his heart.

"Continue? Nothing can ever take you from this place. Your Mission is completed," Sal said.

Something must be wrong. He tried to read Brother David's expression.

"Act quickly Sal. God gives and takes in his own time," Brother David said. His words were slow and deliberative. Sal began to imagine the worst.

"Are you ill? Why speak this way?" Sal said. Did he suffer from some sickness? Sal could not stand to have another friend taken from him. No matter how much love he felt for Maria Theresa, he could not think of planning a wedding when his friend faced trouble. He could not think of them being separated again.

"Calm yourself," Brother David said. "Look at all the changes in *Alta California*. You and Paciano have seen for yourself how vast this territory is. Farther Serra saw its promise years ago before he passed on to his reward in heaven, God rest his soul."

"Yes, but you and others carry on. I've seen the other Missions and your church is complete now," Sal said. Did Brother David resign himself to fate, after all these years of teaching Sal to trust God. What happened?

"It was never my Mission. Spain is withdrawing support for all its Missions in the New

World, Sal. They will also recall the military," Brother David said. "The bear meat has helped us through one famine. You yourself have made this possible."

"At *El Señor* Duran's *Rancho* I saw more Mexican soldiers and government agents. They talk like they expect authority in *Alta California*. Is Spain's rule truly over?" Sal said. He had always cursed his King and felt he was Spanish by blood alone. Would he be abandoned once again?

"*México* even wants to replace the Spanish clergy with its own native-born friars. How long can I last?" Brother David said. He looked around the beloved hilltop Mission as if he already packed his memories for the long trip home.

"If you must leave, I'll go home with you," Sal said. His heart broke.

"No Sal, this is your new home," Brother David said. He scooped a handful of sandy soil and held it out toward Sal.

"Don't leave me," Sal said. He could see his mother dying, his father walking away with another family. Like a child, he pushed away Brother David's handful of *Alta California* soil.

"Stay and be married," Brother David said.

"Tell me this one thing, is *El Señor* Duran a Mexican citizen or a Spaniard?"

Sal wondered, why would the Brother judge the Duran family this way? What an odd question to ask at such a moment? "Maria's father? What difference does it make?" Sal said. "He is from *México*; he received his land grant last year."

"Then, by all means, marry Maria Theresa," Brother David said. "Salvador Tenorio you've become an honorable man." He took a step back and held his small cross above Sal's head. "You earned your place here. Maria Theresa's dowry will make you an official land owner. Her love will give you strength to be the man you wish to be. God's work continues in you."

It felt like a kind of baptism, or confirmation, or one of those rites Sal paid so little attention to in his youth. No longer a boy, no longer out for his own fortune alone. He saw a larger purpose, a larger life than he could have ever hoped for. Brother David fumbled with a tattered package. He handed some rag covered object to Sal.

"As a wedding gift I will leave you a special set of candlesticks, the ones with the special twisted cross, for your evening prayers," Brother

David said. "Promise to remember God, just as God promises to remember you."

COMING NEXT:

The Laredo School for Young Ladies: A Place for Secrets

By Anita Perez Ferguson

YOUNG ADULT – HISTORIC FICTION – ADVENTURE

He lurked around the *hacienda* patio. Alicia Ortega spied on Captain Harris as she pretended to tidy Mamà's altar in the *sala*. Like a fox circling the hen house, she thought. She replaced the candles around Mother Mary who whispered a warning, "*Cuídate, Mija*," through a thin glaze of wax.

Harris, and other buccaneers, off-loaded black market cargo at Papà's secret harbor, *Refugio*, in *Alta California*. By 1805 this refuge from Spanish duty fees was not truly a secret to anyone. Even Padre Romo from the Mission bargained at the Ortega's makeshift dock for linens, silks and ornaments.

"That scoundrel, Harris, is looking for your sister, Clara," Nina said. She swept ashes from the hearth below the altar. "I've seen them all week, whispering and making marks on your Mamà's parchments." Nina was the Mission-trained housekeeper to the Ortega family. She endured endless chores by gossiping and day dreaming with Alicia. The girls grew up together, fifteen lonely years at *Rancho Refugio*.

Captain Harris was no dreamer. He was after something. Alicia intended to guard all the Ortega family treasures and secrets from him. "*Refugio* is not like any port around Boston, Manchester or Salem where we ran our cargo ships when my father was in charge," Harris told anyone who would listen. "My father was all business, everything had to be shipshape and by the book. When my brother inherited the business, I knew there would be no place for me. That's when I headed south around the horn of South America looking for a place of my own."

CPSIA information can be obtained
at www.ICGtesting.com
Printed in the USA
FSHW011640010921
84398FS